The Guns of Easter

Gerard Whelan

THE O'BRIEN PRESS
DUBLIN

First published 1996 by The O'Brien Press Ltd,
12 Terenure Road East, Rathgar, Dublin 6, Ireland.
Tel: +353 1 4923333; Fax: +353 1 4922777
E-mail: books@obrien.ie; Website: www.obrien.ie
Reprinted 1997, 1998 (twice), 1999, 2000, 2001, 2002, 2004 (twice), 2006, 2007,
2009, 2010, 2011, 2012, 2014, 2015.

ISBN: 978-0-86278-449-2

18 20 23 22 21 19
15 17 19 18 16

Typesetting, editing, layout, design: The O'Brien Press Ltd
Printed and bound by Norhaven Paperback A/S, Denmark.
The paper in this book is produced using pulp from managed forests

The O'Brien Press receives assistance from

Contents

Dedication

This book is dedicated to Niamh Lynch, Birr, County Offaly,
and to Oisín Barrett, Oceanside, Ca, USA.

Acknowledgements

My wife, Maria Ziere, did endless printouts of this book;
Íde ní Laoghaire, at O'Brien, trimmed its worst excesses.
Without them the manuscript would be
sitting in a shoebox somewhere.

PART ONE: A BOY AND HIS CITY

1

JIMMY CONWAY

IT WAS STILL ONLY TWILIGHT in the streets outside, but in the high hallway of the tenement house night had fallen long ago. There were no lights in the hall, and it was pitch black.

Jimmy Conway had often made this journey in the dark. In some ways he preferred it, because you couldn't see the shabbiness and dirt. He moved quickly and quietly now up the dangerous stairs, avoiding the missing treads and the loose banisters. Sometimes drunken people slept on the stairs, and you'd have to step over them; but tonight Jimmy heard no snores, and was glad of it. He kept going until he stood outside the door of his own home. Then he stopped and stood silently, looking and listening.

There was no sound from inside, and no light showed around the ill-fitting door. That was good. Ma was due to go and see Mrs Doyle tonight about getting some work. Sometimes the nuns in the convent gave Mrs Doyle a bit of washing to do. It was the only money the Doyles had, but if there was a big batch of laundry Mrs Doyle would let Jimmy's Ma do some of it. The work wasn't regular, and the money wasn't good, but every penny was welcome.

It was more than a matter of money. 'You can't trust just anybody with the holy nuns' washing,' Mrs Doyle would say. 'But you could trust Lily Conway with your own life, because there's no more respectable nor decent woman going.'

Hearing her say this was worth gold to Jimmy's Ma. It helped her keep her head up, she said, when her heart was dragging.

Ma's heart seemed to be dragging a lot lately. It was the reason Jimmy was glad she wasn't home. He wouldn't put it past some of the local gossips to come and tell her lies about him just for the sake of passing scandal. Some of them had nothing better to do.

Obviously no gossips had come. If Ma had heard about the old man, and thought that Jimmy was involved, it would have broken her heart. She'd have stayed home to wait for him, and he'd have heard her crying before he even went in. She wouldn't beat him, but the crying would be worse. When she cried he felt like begging her to hit him instead: it would hurt less.

There was no lock on the door. Jimmy opened it silently and stepped inside. The single big window was a pale rectangle in the darkness. It was a handsome window, a relic of the times when these houses had been the homes of the gentry. One of the windowpanes was cracked, but at least it wasn't broken, and there were heavy curtains that kept out the worst of the cold in winter. Many of the neighbours had windows that were full of holes, with maybe bits of paper stuck over them; and some had no curtains at all.

Jimmy heard the breathing of his sleeping sisters. He crept towards the mattress in the corner where Sarah was already lying. From the big bed in the opposite corner Josie made a noise in her sleep. Jimmy stopped, but Josie was only dreaming. When she was quiet again he went on.

He knew exactly where to put his feet, and sidestepped the hole in the rotten board by the corner of the mattress. Then he eased off his boots, crept in beside Sarah and pulled the old coats that were his bedcovers over him. He relaxed a bit then, safe for now at least, and lay on his back in the dark, thinking.

By the standards of many of his friends, Jimmy's home was more than comfortable. True, it was only a single room, and there were those places on the floor where adults shouldn't walk because the rotting boards might cave in under their weight. But there were only a few spots like that, and in some homes the whole floor was dangerous. Still his Ma was always going on at the three children, warning them about the holes.

'Mind your feet!' she'd say. 'Watch where you're walking! You don't want to end up like Cissy Kavanagh!'

This was the whole point, of course. Last winter Cissy Kavanagh, one of his friend's sisters, had fallen through the floor of her home into the stairwell and been killed. Kavanaghs' floor must have been very rotten, though, because Cissy hadn't weighed much at all. She'd been seven years old, and very thin.

Jimmy's Ma was always worrying about how awful their home was, even when Jimmy pointed out to her that they were very lucky compared to plenty of the people they knew. Even the cracks that showed in the plaster in one corner of their ceiling weren't too bad; the Twomeys, who lived on the floor above, had one big piece of their ceiling fall in on them during a storm last January. Rain seeping in through the holes in the roof had rotted the plaster. No-one had been hurt that time, but now you could look out through the Twomeys' ceiling and see patches of sky.

There were a lot of very poor people in their part of Dublin. At a political meeting Jimmy had heard a man say that the city had the worst slums in Europe. There were rich people living in the city too, of course, but Jimmy didn't know any of them. You'd see them every day in Sackville Street, shopping and going about their business, but certainly none of them lived around here. Jimmy wasn't even sure how rich people lived, except that they always had enough to eat: you could tell by looking at them.

The whole area where Jimmy lived was crowded with large families living in small spaces. Before Jimmy's Da joined the army they themselves had been much worse off, but even then there'd only been the five of them living in the room. Nowadays there were only four, and three were children – Jimmy, the eldest, was twelve, while Josie was ten and Sarah just six.

When Da came home from the war it would be a tighter fit, but some families had ten or more people living in one room. There had been twelve of the Kavanaghs before Cissie died.

Thinking of his Da always made Jimmy confused. He missed him very much, but he knew that they needed his wages from the army to survive. Da had known that too, but even so he'd hesitated a long time after the war started before joining up.

'Why should I fight their damned wars?' he'd always say. 'Irish and English working men standing in trenches shooting at German working men, while all the time their generals are probably drinking together and laughing at them!'

He'd usually say this when he was discussing politics with Ma's brother Mick. Da was an old trade union man, and blamed the bosses for all of Ireland's troubles. Mick was more of a nationalist; he agreed that the bosses were trouble, but said that the English were the real problem.

'But even if we do get rid of the English the bosses are still there,' Da would say.

'No,' Mick would argue, 'it's the English class system. We could make the bosses change if the English were out of our way.'

'You make it all sound too simple,' Da would tell Mick. 'Come back when you know what you're talking about.'

In the end Da had gone into the army, like many other men. The war had put prices up, and Da hadn't any money to begin with. He'd had no real job for three years, not since taking part in the great strike of 1913 when half the city starved. Finally, one day, he came home looking heartbroken and announced that he'd joined the British army.

'I've enlisted,' he said simply. 'I start training next week.'

Ma was horrified. 'What have you done?' she asked, almost in tears. 'James, what have you gone and done?'

But Da answered her firmly. 'Them childer's faces are thinner every time I look at them, Lily,' he said. 'There's not one employer in town that will give me a job. I'm a marked man since the strike.' Da looked really angry and upset. 'This way, Lil, you'll get a weekly payment from the government. Damn it, woman, can't you understand? You'll be able to eat.'

Ma said it wasn't worth it, that she'd rather they all starved and Da, not wanting to argue with her, just walked out. Afterwards they didn't discuss it again, at least not that Jimmy heard. Anyway, as Da pointed out, it was too late to change anything now. He couldn't back out. A week later he was gone for training, and they began to get the separation allowance. 'Ring money' people called it, referring to a wedding ring. The wedding ring was all that Lily Conway had of her husband James now. He'd been away now for more than a year, in France, fighting the Germans.

Things were a bit easier with the ring money, though it hardly seemed worth losing your Da for. Still, at least there was something to eat most days, and that made a change. Even if the money ran out before the end of the week and you had a hungry weekend, you knew that on Monday there would be money again. It kept you from giving up hope. Lately they'd started to have some hungry weekends, for reasons Jimmy couldn't really understand as Ma was usually very good with money. He felt it had something to do with his aunt Ella.

Jimmy wished more than ever that Da could be here now. The fact that he wasn't made Jimmy the man of the house, and at twelve years of age Jimmy found that hard. The man of the house was supposed to know right from wrong, but Jimmy didn't always find this so simple. And then again even adults couldn't seem to agree on what was right and what wasn't. Uncle Mick, for instance, had been furious with Da for joining the army.

'How can he fight for the British?' Mick asked Ma when he heard the news. 'And for what? For their money.'

This was just after Da went away. A week before, Ma herself had been giving out to Da for signing up, but now she turned on Mick.

'There's food for the children now,' she said. 'That's what that money means to James. That's all that war means to him. He was never out playing soldiers like you and your Citizen Army friends.'

Mick looked insulted but Ma continued, anger in her voice now. 'It's all very well for you, Mick. You're single, and you have no-one to look after, barring yourself. You can afford dreams and high ideas. How long would your dreams last if they were all you had to bring home to a house full of hungry children? Dreams make bad dinners, Mick.'

Suddenly there was a noise in the hall outside and Jimmy recognised the sound of Ma's footsteps. He must let on to be asleep. Would Tommy Doyle have said anything to her? He'd know soon enough.

The door opened and Ma came in. Jimmy heard her cross to the table, then the sound of a match being lit. He opened his eyes a little bit and saw the light of a candle blossoming in the middle of the room. In its glow he saw her standing there, a small woman looking older than her age. He was glad to see she looked no sadder than usual. In fact, she was almost smiling.

He shut his eyes as she looked over towards him, and kept perfectly still. Through lowered eyelids he saw her pick up the candle and come towards himself and Sarah, and he closed his eyes completely. But he had misjudged how exhausted he was by the day's events. He'd hardly closed his eyes before he was suddenly asleep. The last thing he saw in his mind's eye was the sight that he'd been trying not to picture all evening, the terrible purple face of the dead man in the street.

2

AN AUNT AND AN UNCLE

NEXT MORNING JIMMY WAS WOKEN by the sound of his aunt Ella's voice. He lay sleepily listening to her whining.

'But what'll I do, Lily?' Ella said. 'He has no right ...'

'Whisht!' Ma warned. 'The child!'

Jimmy knew that she'd spotted him moving. Now he'd have to get up. He wondered what Ella was doing here so early. Complaining, no doubt; it was all she ever did now.

The two women were sitting by the table. Ella was drinking something from a cup, and Jimmy guessed that his mother had given her sister her own share of the tea again. Ella never seemed to notice that the tea she drank here and the bread she ate came from a very bare larder. This annoyed him, especially since Ella so obviously disliked coming to their poor room at all.

Ella had a home of her own in the south side of the city,

and by all accounts she was quite well off – better than they were at any rate. Sometimes Jimmy wondered why it never struck her to bring a loaf of bread or an ounce of tea with her when she came to visit her sister.

Ella had been visiting quite a lot since last winter. Before that they'd seen little of her since her marriage. She'd married Charlie Fox, a clerk in a brewery, because of his steady job and good prospects. At one time her own family, the Healys, had had money themselves, but those times were long gone. After her marriage, Ella seemed to feel that she was a cut above her relations.

'She thinks she's too good for us now,' Mick used to say. 'She may be my own sister, but she's a stuck up snob.'

As far as Jimmy could make out Mick was right. Even now when Ella called regularly, she let her dislike of their circumstances show. Then there was her whining. She was always having whispered talks with Ma, and during these talks Ella would always end up crying. Worst of all, Jimmy had seen his Ma sometimes pass something secretly to Ella, when she thought he wasn't looking. Jimmy suspected it was money, but he couldn't understand why Ella might need it. What about her husband? Hadn't she always been boasting about his good job? The idea that his Ma might be taking on extra work just so that she could give money to Ella was nearly too much for Jimmy.

Before he'd left, Da told Jimmy to look after his Ma, but Jimmy wasn't sure how to go about it. He decided that the best thing to do was to be good and, when possible, do what Ma told him. If he couldn't help her with the problems of adults, he could at least help by not causing any fresh problems himself.

Thinking about this reminded Jimmy of yesterday. He'd forgotten it in the night. He was suddenly wide awake.

'You let that fellow sleep too much,' Ella said. 'It's bad for him.'

Ella had no children herself, but that didn't stop her giving advice about child rearing. Mind you, Ella hadn't always been such a nuisance. Before she met Charlie Fox she and Jimmy had been quite friendly. She'd never been a complainer then. Marriage had changed Ella a lot, and part of the reason Jimmy disliked her so much now was that he was disappointed in her.

He got up as quickly as he could, with one eye on Ma and Ella. There was no sign of Sarah and Josie. Ma must have sent them out; she often did now when Ella was here. Jimmy hoped to get out himself before Ma even noticed, but as soon as he took a step towards the door she turned and pointed a finger at him.

'You!' she said. 'Wait here. I want to talk to you.' She spoke in what Da used to call her policeman's voice. So she had heard something about yesterday after all. He was sure of it.

Ella was standing up to go, a small, dark woman with a grieving face. Jimmy sat back down on his mattress and kicked his heels. Ma went to the dresser and fumbled in a drawer – getting money, Jimmy thought. He looked around the room, pretending not to notice.

Apart from the dresser there wasn't much to look at. There was very little furniture in the Conways' room. There was the big bed in the far corner, where Ma slept with Josie; when Da was home he shared the bed with Ma, and Josie slept with the other two on the mattress. In the middle of the room was the kitchen table with its battered chairs. The old rocking chair by the fireplace was Ma's. Like the old clock on the mantelpiece, it had come down to her from her own mother. The clock was what Ma called an heirloom. Jimmy ended up staring at it now, as he often did these days. It didn't work any more, but it was still a lovely thing, and even valuable. The casing, Ma said, had pieces of real marble in it, and the metalwork was real brass. There was even silver in it, and pieces of real cut crystal. In the days when they'd had no money Ma had often pawned it with old Mr Meyer, who'd kept a pawnshop in Great Britain Street before he'd been driven out. More than once in those days the clock had kept them from hunger.

'That ould clock,' Da said one time, 'is a better earner nor I am.'

Ella and Ma had a final whisper at the door, then Ella left. Ma turned to Jimmy, who was trying to look innocent.

'James Conway junior,' Ma said, and Jimmy's heart

sank. She only called him James when she was being very serious. 'James Conway junior,' she said again, 'stop looking at that clock and look at me.'

Jimmy looked at her, trying to keep his face as still as the clock's was. To his surprise Ma was almost smiling.

'I'm told,' she said, 'that you did something very responsible yesterday.'

Jimmy gawked at her. What was she on about?

'Kitty Doyle,' Ma said, 'tells me that you kept Tommy from getting involved in a terrible thing.'

Jimmy blushed. Had Tommy Doyle been telling his own Ma the truth about something? It would be against the unwritten rules, but even so Jimmy might be glad of it now. While Jimmy's mind was racing, his mother stood with her hands on her hips, looking at him. 'Well?' she said finally. 'Aren't you going to tell me about it?'

Jimmy wondered where to start. He was still wondering when the door opened and Mick walked in with a scowl on his face.

'Was that our dear sister I saw going down the steps?' he demanded.

'It was Ella, if that's who you mean,' Ma said.

'And how much did she get this time?' Mick said.

Ma clicked her tongue impatiently. 'Mick!' she said. 'Please!'

Mick growled, but said no more. Like Jimmy, Mick tried to help Ma as much as he could. But there were times when Jimmy suspected that Mick, though he might look and sound like an adult, didn't really know how to help any more than Jimmy himself did.

At least twice a week now Mick would call around to ask if everything was all right. Ma would tell him that it was, and this would keep Mick happy. Jimmy suspected that the happiness was really relief, that Mick was glad because he was afraid to hear about problems that he didn't know how to solve. This made Jimmy feel much closer to Mick. At such times Mick seemed less like an uncle than a big brother or a friend.

Mick was only twenty-one, half way between Jimmy's age and Ma's. Jimmy had always been very fond of him. Sometimes when Ma talked about Mick there was something in her voice that made him sound like a child. But she never used that tone when he was there, though she did tend to tease him.

'You came just in time,' she said now. 'Jimmy was just going to tell me about a heroic attack on the army.'

Her voice was sarcastic. Mick looked embarrassed, though he couldn't know what she was talking about. He stared at Jimmy.

'Jimmy!' Ma said. 'Talk!'

Jimmy stammered for a moment and then started. 'It was the Gorgeous Wrecks ...' he began.

'I never liked that name,' Ma butted in. 'Some of them poor old men saw a lot of hardship.'

The Gorgeous Wrecks were officially the Home Defence Force. The Defence Force was made up of British army veterans, many of them very old. Dressed in their uniforms they went on marches around the city carrying their empty rifles. Their belts had big shiny buckles on which the king's name was written in Latin: GEORGIUS REX. Dubliners, looking at these old, broken men strutting proudly along, had nicknamed them the Gorgeous Wrecks.

The boys of Jimmy's area loved to jeer at the old men. It was something to do. In the past Jimmy had always happily joined in, but since Da joined the army Jimmy had been having doubts about it. At least the Wrecks had once been real soldiers – not like the Irish Volunteers, who wanted Ireland to be a separate country, or like Mick's crowd, the Citizen Army, who nowadays seemed to think the same. The Citizen Army was the so-called army of the trade union; a foolish idea, Jimmy thought – trade unions shouldn't have armies.

The Gorgeous Wrecks had at least seen real fighting when they were younger. Some of them had fought the Boers, in the African war that had ended a few years before Jimmy was born. Others had battled the savage Zulus, or the wild Dervish hordes of the Mahdi, who had killed the saintly General Gordon in Khartoum.

'I was down in Abbey Street with some of the lads,' Jimmy said, 'and some of the Gorgeous Wrecks came along ...'

3

THE GORGEOUS WRECKS

THE LADS HAD BEEN STANDING ON THE CORNER of the street daydreaming about finding ways to go to Fairyhouse. The races there were on in a couple of weeks, and they were the biggest event of the season. Several boys boasted that they were going, but of course they were lying. Everybody knew it, too: poor boys like them simply didn't get a chance to go to places like the Fairyhouse races.

They'd grown bored with lying to each other all day and were starting to look around for some fresh devilment when the straggling little group of Home Defence Force veterans came around the corner from Amiens Street.

'Hey!' Billy Moran said. 'It's the Wrecks!'

'Parade!' shouted someone. 'Parade! The army's here!'

Following army parades was great fun. Not that the Gorgeous Wrecks really counted as an army parade, but they were better than nothing. There was, of course, only one real army, and that was the army of His Royal Highness, King George V. Nothing could match the thrill of marching behind the real army. Once, Jimmy had heard, British soldiers had dressed in red and green and blue; but even now, in khaki, they were the most glamorous thing he knew.

When the cavalry rode on parade, in their dress uniforms, the sheer glory of it was enough to make your heart skip a beat. You wanted nothing more than to be one of them, to ride along knowing that the people watching were saying to one another: 'Oh look, look at the soldier on his fine horse. Isn't he grand?'

The army bands too still wore bright uniforms on parades and recruiting marches, and since the war began there seemed to be a parade or a recruiting march almost every day. When the bands marched, all the boys would fall in behind them and try to match their steps. The people would gather to watch the marching band, and if you were marching behind them then you could almost believe that it was you that the people were watching.

The real soldiers never seemed to mind boys marching behind them, but all the other groups who marched were more sensitive about it. It was as though the boys' presence reminded them that they weren't real soldiers at all.

Jimmy was standing with Tommy Doyle. Tommy had been quiet all week. His sister, Alice, was very sick, and he was worried about her. Now when he saw the Gorgeous Wrecks he seemed to cheer up.

Jimmy himself had mixed feelings as he watched the old men coming closer. He found it strange to think that once these men had been young and proud and straight like his father. Once too, long before that, they had been young boys like himself. Even more strange, one day he himself would be old like them, with white hair or else no hair at all, and a face filled with blotches and wrinkles.

As the old soldiers passed the boys started to fall in behind them, marching too. Billy Moran and Andy Moore had sticks that they let on were rifles, and the rest of the boys just swung their arms.

Tommy Doyle grabbed Jimmy's arm.

'Let's go,' he said. 'You can be sergeant.'

Jimmy hesitated. This was bound to end up with the old men annoyed. He knew Ma wouldn't like him to jeer at them. Just the other day, too, he'd heard Tommy's Ma say that her own da had been in the army, and that she'd hate to think of chiselers laughing at him if he'd been in the Home Defence. But he'd died in Africa, defending the Empire; an Irishman fighting for the other side had shot him.

'Wait,' Jimmy said, and held his friend back.

Tommy wasn't the type of boy to wait for anything, but he waited for Jimmy's sake – after all it was only the Wrecks.

As the old men marched past them, followed by the boys, the usual thing started to happen: a few of the veterans started to give out to the boys, who in turn began to taunt them. Then one old soldier got really upset. He stopped marching and turned on his tormentors, trying to clout them. But the man wasn't very fast on his feet, and the boys were. They formed a jeering ring around him, staying just out of his reach, while Jimmy and Tommy looked on silently.

The march itself was quickly in confusion. Some of the old soldiers in front, deaf or half-doting, kept on marching; others stopped and looked around at the uproar.

The angry old man still stood in the middle of the jeering ring. He'd started by talking about queen and country, but now he was cursing the boys wildly. He threw his rifle on the ground. His face got more and more red. There was something not right about the way he was going on, something extreme. The jeering boys seemed to notice nothing odd about their victim. Passersby were stopping now to watch the fun.

'Jimmy!' Tommy Doyle said. He was staring at the old man.

Suddenly the old fellow stopped in mid-word. For a moment he was silent, then he started crying. A jeering cheer went up from the boys around him.

'For shame!' said a passerby, and Jimmy felt like agreeing with him. Watching the unfortunate old man, he did feel ashamed.

With no warning, the old man fell down. He put his hands to his chest, looked wildly around him and then keeled over. As he fell he made a terrible sound, a sound that had no name that Jimmy knew.

A woman screamed. The old man lay on the street, his face a terrible purple colour. Spittle ran out of his mouth.

His eyes were wide open, staring, white. The pupils had rolled up into his head, like the eyes of the dead man Josie had found frozen one winter outside in the yard.

People gathered around the fallen man. Through their legs Jimmy could see him lying there. He knew instantly that the old soldier had had some kind of attack, that he wouldn't be getting up again, that the jeering had killed him.

Jimmy stood and stared. The whole incident had taken less than five minutes, and here was a man dead in the street. Jimmy couldn't believe it. He wasn't thinking straight.

The most sensible thought came to Tommy Doyle.

'Jimmy!' Tommy whispered urgently in his ear. 'Let's go. Now!'

'But we did nothing!' Jimmy said.

'That never stopped us getting blamed before,' Tommy said. 'Come on!'

The boys who'd actually done the jeering had vanished. People were starting to look around for the youngsters who'd caused the old man's attack. Jimmy and Tommy took to their heels and within seconds they'd disappeared into the familiar streets around home, where no-one would notice them.

Even now, the next day, Jimmy found it impossible to explain to Ma and Mick how he'd felt after the old man died. There was a feeling of guilt, even though he hadn't taunted the old man. He kept telling himself that he hadn't been involved, but it was no good.

Still, Ma was looking at him with pride on her face. 'The man's name was O'Brien,' she said quietly. 'Mrs Doyle saw it in the paper. He had medals for bravery in some war or another, I don't know which. When she asked Tommy if he'd been near Abbey Street yesterday he told her all about how you'd kept him out of trouble. "God bless that child," says she to me. "God bless that child and the parents that raised him."'

Jimmy felt that Ma was making a fuss about something that was really quite small. He hadn't really done anything much. Yet he loved her approval and he loved to see her happy. He knew from her smile just how happy she was, and when she turned to her brother Jimmy knew from the twinkle in her eye that she was going to tease him.

'Well, Mick?' Ma said.

Mick looked at her. He never noticed the twinkle, and always reacted to her teasing.

'Well what?' he said.

'Aren't you ashamed?'

Mick's jaw dropped open with surprise. 'Ashamed of what?' he asked.

'It's the kind of rebel crowd you're involved with that has the children acting like this,' Ma said. 'Jeering poor harmless old men and giving them fits.'

Mick positively spluttered with indignation. He was not very good at expressing himself, and the unfairness of the accusation left him speechless. Safe now himself, Jimmy enjoyed watching the discomfort that washed across his uncle's face.

'Lily!' Mick spluttered. 'Them kids would follow a herd of cows to the docks if the cows were only marching! They follow the army bands and the Home Defence and everybody else! For God's sake, they even follow the Volunteers!'

Jimmy was surprised that Mick had managed to get so much out. Ma was looking at her brother with no expression on her face, but Jimmy saw the ghost of a smile around her mouth. Mick was so upset he was almost shaking.

'Excuse me,' Ma said. '*My* Jimmy didn't follow anyone. *And* he kept Tommy Doyle out of trouble too. Isn't it a pity there's not more like him, Mrs Doyle said, that might grow into men that would mind their own business and stop trying to right the wrongs of the whole world!'

Jimmy knew that this was a dig at Mick's involvement in the union and the Citizen Army. Mick was a great admirer of the union leader, James Connolly. Connolly was something called a socialist, and Mick often called himself a socialist too, although when you asked him he could never quite explain what a socialist was.

This final dig was too much for Mick. He had a short temper, though his bad moods never lasted long and he always regretted them. Now he tried again to make some smart answer, but instead after a minute he gave up.

'I'll tell ya, Lil,' he said, 'I don't know about righting the wrongs of the world, but I surely won't answer for all the sins of the world!'

And he turned on his heel and stamped out of the room, banging the door after him. They heard him clattering down the stairs, catch his foot on the loose step above the first landing and curse. Ma couldn't keep a straight face any more. She burst out laughing and grabbed hold of Jimmy. He clung to her warmth, relief flooding through him. Ma's laughter was the nicest sound in the world. When he heard her laughing he felt that he must be doing what Da had asked, and looking after her.

'Oh Jimmy,' she said to him, 'you're the grandest son that a mother could have!'

'What about poor Mick?' Jimmy asked her. He knew it was hard not to tease Mick sometimes, but he was fond of his uncle.

Ma laughed again.

'That big eejit!' she said. 'He'll be back. Don't you worry. And when he comes back maybe we'll even find out why he came in the first place.'

'He came to see if you were all right,' Jimmy said. 'The way he always does.'

Ma swung him away from her but didn't let go. Her face was happy.

'But, sure, how would I not be all right,' she said, 'when I have the grandest son in Ireland looking after me?'

4

THE THINKING GAME

AFTERWARDS JIMMY'S MA WENT OFF TO DOYLES' to see whether the laundry had arrived yet from the nuns. Josie and Sarah were there already, visiting Tommy's sister Alice. Alice was a pale girl who always seemed to be suffering from one illness or another. She'd been very sick with a fever for a week now.

'Why don't you stay at home and amuse yourself?' Ma told Jimmy before she went out. 'I won't be back for a couple of hours, and the girls can wait for me. It's not often that you have the place to yourself.'

This suited Jimmy very well. He'd been spending more time at home lately though in his heart he really preferred to be out in the streets with his friends. With them he could do all the things that boys like to do. The problem was that sometimes the things the boys did got you in trouble. Jimmy, when he remembered, tried to avoid getting involved with things like that. But mostly he just forgot, and then Ma was hurt.

Sometimes Jimmy managed to remember and stay out of trouble. That was really all that had happened yesterday, however much Ma and Kitty Doyle had made

30

out of it. But avoiding involvement was hard sometimes too. If the other boys noticed, they might think you were afraid, and they would call you a sissy or a German. These were very bad things to be called, and so sometimes Jimmy ended up doing things he really didn't want to do. So he tended to spend much more time at home now, avoiding temptation. It was the easiest way in the end.

When Ma left, Jimmy sat in her rocking chair by the fire and again looked up at the old clock on the mantelpiece. The clock was part of a new game that he'd found lately. He called it the thinking game.

The thinking game wasn't a game like football or chasing. It was a game that you played on your own. What you did was to sit and make up exciting stories for yourself. If you imagined hard enough, you could be anything in the thinking game. It was great fun, because when your adventures were all in your mind you could do things that you could never do in real life. As well as that, of course, the things you did couldn't get you into trouble. That was a definite bonus.

When Jimmy was playing the thinking game he didn't like to be disturbed. This was difficult when there were other people in the room, but if he thought hard enough he could eventually ignore them. It was like having a little private room in your head where you could go and play. Once you were in the little room you could be anything and anywhere you liked. The problem was getting to that little room in the first place.

Gradually Jimmy had found a way to help him reach the little room and start his game. The first thing he did was to concentrate on something in the big room that was his home. He'd stare at the thing and think about it until the noises of his sisters' play faded, and even the noises from the street outside sounded as if they came from very far away.

Sometimes people thought there was something wrong with him.

'What's he staring like that for?' Ella would ask, forgetting her troubles for a moment. 'Is he sick?'

'He's just thinking,' Ma would say, with a note of pride in her voice.

'Thinking!' Ella would answer, as though thinking were some awful crime. 'Why isn't he out playing like a normal young fellow?'

'He plays enough. Let him think. It's a pity more men wouldn't try it now and then.'

And Ella, busy with her own problems, would soon go back to telling Ma about them in a choked whisper.

It didn't do to start your thinking by looking at just anything. Most of the things in the room were far too ordinary. The mattresses were old and sagging, the rest of the furniture chipped and scratched. If you looked closely at such things your daydreams would be scratched and sagging too, and that was no use: that was just like the world you saw around you every day.

The best thing in the room to start Jimmy thinking was what Ella called 'that old clock'.

The numbers on the clock's face were in the form of letters, like the letters after the king's name that were really a number. That was how the Romans had written numbers, Da told Jimmy one time. The Romans were people who'd been around a long time ago. They'd never come to Ireland, but once they'd owned Britain just as Britain now owned Ireland.

Long ago, when the clock had stopped, its hands had been pointing at five to twelve – XI to XII, the Roman numerals on the face said. Five minutes to midnight, Ma would say when she was telling the girls the ghost stories they loved. It was a joke in the house, the fact that the clock always showed the same time. Jimmy could remember Da coming in at night and looking at the clock in mock surprise.

'Janey mack!' he'd say. 'Is that the time? I'm late!'

And the children would laugh at his foolishness, while Da let on not to know what they were laughing at. Even when there was no money, Da could always make them laugh. In the old days they all missed the clock whenever it was pawned. The old pawnbroker, Mr Meyer, was an admirer of fine objects. He liked Ma, and he collected clocks. One time he offered Ma five pounds for it, to add it to his collection. But Ma explained to him that it was her heirloom. She'd got it from her own mother, who'd got it from hers. It was a reminder of the time, long ago, when her family had money for such things. So Ma refused to sell the clock, though she'd been very tempted.

Mr Meyer always gave Ma a few shillings when she came to pawn the clock, even though she wouldn't sell it. He liked to look at it, he said; and he could be sure that she'd always find money to redeem the pledge. Once, when she was late with the money, she'd gone to the pawnshop with Jimmy and she'd been almost in tears.

'I suppose it's yours now by law,' she said to old Meyer. 'I should have sold it to you when I had the chance.'

Mr Meyer was horrified. 'My dear lady,' he said, in his high voice with the heavy foreign accent. 'How could you think me so cruel? I know how much you love that clock. How could I cheat you of it?'

Mr Meyer's shop was gone now. It had closed shortly after the start of the war. A mob of people threatened him, and threw stones through his windows. They thought Mr Meyer was a German, and they didn't like Germans because they were at war with Germany. They'd been told that Germans were cruel to defenceless people.

In fact Mr Meyer wasn't a German at all. He was from Russia, but had lived in Austria. He was Jewish, and had left Austria because many people there didn't like Jews. This was fine by him, he said, because he didn't especially like Austrians himself. But he hadn't tried to explain any of this to the people in Dublin who threw stones through the windows of his shop.

'You cannot explain things to a mob,' he told Ma when she said how sorry she was about it all. 'In any country, a mob is just a mob.'

Mr Meyer took his savings and retired to some place over in the west of Ireland, where he lived happily now by the sea. One day Ma had met him in Sackville Street, when he was up shopping in Dublin. He told her he was very happy in his new life. Around where he lived now, he said, the people were in favour of Irish freedom. They hated the British, and because the Germans were fighting the British they loved the Germans. They were very friendly to Mr Meyer because they too thought he was German.

Mr Meyer didn't try to explain himself to these people either. He thought it was funny that whether he was loved or hated, it was always for being something that he really wasn't.

'I have lived now for sixty-five years,' he told Ma, giving her sixpence for the children. 'I have lived in six countries and I have learned only one great lesson in my life: people are crazy. Teach your children that lesson and you will save them a great deal of trouble.'

The clock that Mr Meyer liked to look at had fine crystal glass on its face. When you looked at it, with its glass and metal gleaming in the light, it held your attention. It seemed to belong to another time and place, somewhere lighter and sunnier than the world Jimmy knew. It made you think of knights and dragons and big houses and princesses, such as Jimmy had seen once when his father took him to the Christmas pantomime in the days when they'd had money for such things.

Sometimes the stories that Jimmy told himself in his thinking game even included the clock itself. Then the clock became the priceless treasure that he – Sir Jimmy of Dublin – guarded with a flaming lance from evil knights and great winged dragons that breathed fire and smoke. What a dragon might want with a clock Jimmy didn't know, but then that was one of the great things about the thinking game: you didn't have to worry about awkward little questions. In the thinking game you were the boss, and things were simple.

Jimmy sat in the rocking chair and stared at the clock. He tried to think of nothing, either good or bad. Soon the noises from the street outside were fading and he was getting closer to the little room in his head. But then the door of the real room opened and Jimmy was suddenly back in the shabby world of reality. He blinked uncertainly. It was like waking up from a deep sleep. When he looked around he saw his uncle Mick standing in the doorway staring at him. He looked miserable.

5

UNCLE MICK

MICK GLANCED AROUND THE ROOM. 'Where's your Ma?' he asked.

'Gone up to Doyles',' Jimmy said.

Mick came in and closed the door behind him.

'I lost my temper earlier on,' he said. 'Your Ma does that to me sometimes.'

'Sure she does it on purpose,' Jimmy said. 'You know that. You're worse to let her annoy you.'

Mick threw his cap on the table and sat down. He scratched his head and tried to smile his special big smile at Jimmy. Whenever Mick smiled his big smile Jimmy could feel his own lips smiling back even if he wasn't in a very good mood. Mick had that effect on a lot of people. Nearly everyone liked him except, Jimmy sometimes thought, Ella; but then Ella didn't seem to like anybody, so she didn't really count.

Today there seemed to be something wrong with Mick's big smile. It was forced and hollow.

'If she's up in Doyles' then she'll know my news already,' he said.

'What is it?' Jimmy said. 'What's wrong?'

'Wrong?' Mick looked upset. 'I don't know anymore what's wrong or right, Jimmy. Paddy Doyle is after joining up.'

'Tommy's Da? You must be joking. He's a mad rebel. He always says he'll die before he takes the king's shilling. That's what he calls joining up, Tommy says.'

'Oh I know what Paddy always says, Jimmy. He had rows with your Da after he enlisted and told him what he thought of him.'

'Then how could he join the army?'

Mick shook his head. 'It's the daughter – though I suppose that was only the last straw.'

'Alice? What about her? I know she was sick again.'

'She very nearly died, Jimmy, and they hadn't a halfpenny to get a proper doctor. Paddy said he hadn't even the money to bury her. She'd be put in a paupers' grave without even a headstone over her. He could stand the poverty himself, but he couldn't stand the effect on the childer. That's how they get you, he said.'

'But there's work to be had now, since the war started. You always get work.'

Mick was a casual labourer, which meant that he didn't have a steady job; but he was young and strong, and so he could always get work. Sometimes he worked on the docks, loading or unloading ships. Sometimes too he worked in the stables in Guinness's brewery, where Ella's husband Charlie was a clerk. Mick helped to look after the great horses that pulled the brewery carts. He had a natural talent with horses. Once he'd taken Jimmy along to see the carts being loaded. Being so close to the big animals made Jimmy a bit nervous, but Mick handled them with ease.

The war had been good for work because so much material had to be shipped to the army in France, and of course there were less workers around because so many men had joined the army in the first place. When Jimmy first heard this he thought that maybe now Da could leave the army and come home, because at last there would be work for him too. But Ma told him that this wasn't possible – you didn't just leave the army like a man might leave a job he didn't like.

'Besides,' she said, 'the bosses here still hate him. He was too much of a trade union man.'

Jimmy remembered that Paddy Doyle had been a union man as well – he'd been very involved in the 1913 strike, like Da. If Da was on an employer's blacklist then Paddy Doyle would be on it too. It was awful to think that all these men were still paying for something that had happened years ago. All they'd ever wanted was a decent wage.

'I met Paddy in the pub last night,' Mick said. 'He was very drunk. He was so miserable I thought Alice was after dying. When I asked him what was wrong he looked up at me and he said, "I'm a dead man, Mick Healy. Worse, I'm a hypocrite." He's convinced he'll die in the war and he even thinks he deserves to for joining the army at all.'

'But if he's sure he'll be killed,' Jimmy said, 'what's the use of joining up?'

'While he's alive the family will get the separation money,' Mick said. 'If he dies they'll get a pension. He thinks it's all he can do for them now – give his life. And he hates himself for the way he's doing it.'

'But ...' Suddenly Jimmy stopped talking. He'd been struck by a terrible thought. 'Mick,' he said, 'is that what Da is doing? Is he gone out there expecting to die too?'

Mick looked completely miserable. 'I don't know,' he said. 'It could well be. Your Ma was right, Jimmy. She said I didn't understand. Listening to Paddy opened my eyes to some things. He talked about your Da last night. "James Conway is the bravest man I ever met," Paddy said. "When he saw what he had to do, he just did it. And here am I driven to it in the end, and complaining about it." It was terrible to listen to him, Jimmy.'

But Jimmy wasn't listening to Mick any more. His mind was whirling. 'Mick,' he said, 'do you think Ma knows this?'

'I don't know. Your Da would never say it to her, but she's not a fool.'

In his mind Jimmy saw the dreams he'd had of himself as a soldier for England, dressed in khaki and dug into the trenches fighting for a good cause. He saw the dreams shatter and disappear, and there was nothing in their place except the reality of hunger and poverty and dirty streets, and people doing terrible things because they had no choices.

'Mick,' he said, really wanting to know. 'Are there any good causes? Ones worth dying for?'

Mick thought before answering. Jimmy knew that he was thinking of his own activities in the Citizen Army, of all his old talk about freeing Ireland and about justice for the poor workers. When he finally answered, he sounded every bit as uncertain as Jimmy felt.

'I don't know any more, Jimmy,' Mick said. 'I used to think so, but now I just don't know.'

6

FAIRYHOUSE DREAMS

THE NEW IDEAS ABOUT HIS FATHER drove all the good feelings out of Jimmy's head. After Mick left he tried to start his thinking game again, but it was no use. All that he could think about was Da, going off to a war that he didn't believe in, in a uniform he despised, so that his family could have some money. This was the simple reality, not just for Da but for many others. Only his own foolish dreams of glory had kept Jimmy from seeing the truth before.

He tried to hide his misery from Ma when she got back with the washing. She could see that there was something wrong, but she decided not to pry. He must, she thought, be thinking about that poor old man yesterday.

Lily Conway had not been as surprised as her brother and son to hear that Paddy Doyle had joined the army. He was an honourable man and a good husband. He'd tried in every way to provide for his family, but the small world of Dublin had kept him from doing it. Now he was taking the only way out. Her own husband had done the same thing. She hadn't liked it, but people like them didn't have many choices. Lily could see no dishonour in it. If she'd heard Paddy Doyle calling himself a hypocrite she'd have been shocked.

Almost a week passed with Jimmy in the same awful mood. He didn't go out, just sat staring out the window. It began to get on Ma's nerves. She'd tried more than once to talk to him, to find out what was wrong, but got no good from the attempts.

In the course of that week she hadn't talked to her brother Mick. Ella called twice, but that was little cause for rejoicing. Ella was so wrapped up in her own troubles now that she hardly even listened when anyone else spoke. She just wanted her own complaining to be heard.

Alice Doyle recovered from her fever. It had already been breaking on the day Lily collected the laundry, otherwise she wouldn't have let the two girls up to

Doyles' at all. These fevers were always around in the cramped and dirty conditions of the slums. They went through the underfed children like wildfire, and always killed a few as they went. There was hardly a household she knew that hadn't had a dead child at some time; her own family had, she knew, been very lucky.

It was Mick who brought the change in Jimmy in the end, hard though that was to credit. Mick always wanted to help, and he did try his best; but he never knew how, and always seemed to get things wrong. This time though he came up trumps, and with a few words transformed her son from the moping nuisance he'd become into the most radiant boy in Dublin.

It happened exactly a week after the affair of the Gorgeous Wrecks. The day started like any other recent one, with the girls squabbling and Jimmy sitting looking at the floor. Lily Conway, beset with worries of her own that she tried to hide from the children, was counting her coppers to see whether there was enough money for an ounce of tea and a loaf of bread.

She stopped in the middle of counting and looked at the three children, the light of her life. She thought of her husband, and wondered where he was at that exact moment. Then she made herself stop thinking about him, as she always did, because at this exact moment he might be dying or terribly injured.

The door opened and Mick sailed in. He was wearing

the huge smile that everyone liked. When he walked into a room smiling like that the whole place seemed to light up.

Lily was delighted to see him in this mood. Though he hadn't called during the week, she'd seen him in the street a couple of times; but he'd looked every bit as miserable as Jimmy, and she hadn't stopped to talk. She'd felt she had enough miserable people to deal with, and was having problems coping herself.

Now all that seemed to have changed. Mick came in smiling and whistling.

'Howya, Lil?' he said. 'And how are my dear nieces?'

The girls ran over and hugged him. Jimmy, though, barely reacted. Mick escaped the girls and went over to the rocking chair.

'I say, old fellow,' he said to Jimmy in a mock English accent, 'have I got news for you.'

Jimmy looked up at him moodily. What news could Mick have? Nothing good, certainly. Jimmy said nothing.

'You never mind that sulky young fella,' Ma said. 'We want to know, even if he doesn't.'

'I'll tell you so,' said Mick. 'Though it concerns Jimmy more than the rest of you. The thing is, I've got some work at the end of next week.'

Jimmy shrugged. That was hardly very exciting.

'Do you remember,' said Mick, 'when I was working in the stables in the brewery?'

'Of course,' Ma said.

'Jim?' Mick said. 'You remember the day that I took you to work with me?'

Jimmy grunted.

'Do you remember a man there by the name of Tandy? He was very taken with you.'

'That was the man that said you should work with horses all the time,' Jimmy said. 'He gave me sixpence.' It was the sort of thing that you'd remember.

'The very man,' Mick said. 'Well, I met Mr Tandy the other day, and he said he could give me a couple of days' work.'

'Grand,' said Jimmy. 'Good for you.'

'At Fairyhouse,' said Mick.

Jimmy looked at him.

'For the races,' Mick said.

Jimmy straightened in his seat.

'And he said,' went on Mick, 'that I should bring along that bright nephew of mine to help me. "I'm sure," he said, "the chiseler'd like to see the horses." '

Jimmy's mouth dropped open. 'Oh Mick,' he said. 'Are you codding?'

It didn't seem possible for Mick's smile to get any bigger. 'It's true all right, young Jimmy,' he said. 'That's if you want to go.'

From her seat by the table Ma watched the transformation in Jimmy. His face lit up instantly, like the sun coming out from behind a cloud. The miserable thoughts of the last week were driven away. Nothing else could have had such an instant effect. Fairyhouse was special – so special that the thought of really going there left no room in Jimmy's head for anything else at all.

In his mind's eye Jimmy saw himself already at the races, helping Mick in the stables, chatting to jockeys and to the rich men who owned the winning horses.

Not one of the boys Jimmy knew had ever actually been to Fairyhouse. Paddy Doyle had gone there once, years and years ago. Tommy Doyle still boasted of the fact, and described all his father had seen as if he'd seen it himself. That was all very well … but to go there yourself! That was like a story that Jimmy might invent in the thinking game. No, though: even Jimmy would never let his imagination go that far. It was one thing to dream of killing dragons, but it was unthinkable that anyone would ever ask you to go to Fairyhouse for the races.

'Well?' he heard Mick asking, as though from far away. Mick's voice sounded amused. 'Do you want to go or not?'

He must know how foolish the question was. Of course Jimmy wanted to go! Already he could imagine the scene in his mind's eye. The races were on Easter Monday – in a week's time. Dublin would be awful then, closed for the holiday. The Spring Show would be starting, but that would be miles away in Ballsbridge, and it would be mostly farmers and country people who came to see it. All the city people who could get away would be gone, and any who could afford it would be heading for the races.

Fairyhouse would be packed with all the grandest people. Jimmy would see all the great gentlemen, and the army officers in their best dress uniforms, strolling with their ladies on their arms. They would be the kind of people who lived in big houses, with five rooms for each person instead of five people to each room. They would have servants to do all their work for them. They would eat strange foods that these servants prepared for them, in special rooms that were kept only to eat in.

Jimmy knew that there really were people who lived like this, though he wasn't clear about the details of their lives. He only knew that they were magnificent and rich. When they joined the army they became officers and rode horses, and gave orders to ordinary men like Da. They were better than people like Jimmy and his family, in some strange way that Jimmy could never quite understand. Sometimes he even thought that it was simply a case of their having more money; but he always felt that there was something vaguely sinful about thinking this, and mentioned it to no-one.

Whatever the case might be, there was no doubt that Fairyhouse would be crammed with such glamorous people. Jimmy would see them all, and maybe some of them would even talk to him. When he got back afterwards, the other boys would beg him to tell them all about it. He'd be a hero then, a boy who'd had a great adventure. His friends would boast to other boys about him. These other boys would look at him in awe, thinking how normal he looked for someone who'd had such great adventures. Meanwhile Jimmy, the soul of modesty, would try his best to act like just another human being, though inside himself he'd be burning with pride.

Jimmy was so excited that he almost forgot to breathe. It would all be grand, better than walking behind fifty regimental bands at once.

'If you think you'll be up to the journey,' Mick said mockingly, 'we'll be leaving on Saturday evening, and we won't be back maybe till Tuesday.'

Up to the journey? Jimmy blinked at his uncle's smiling face. Did Mick think he'd fall asleep on the way? Why, Jimmy doubted that he'd get any sleep at all for the next week.

He stammered a quick acceptance. He couldn't express his gratitude properly. It was just too big for words. The girls played with their dolls on the floor. Ma sat smiling.

Suddenly Jimmy couldn't contain his joy for another second. It seemed to burst out of him. He gave a great whoop of happiness that made the adults laugh and made his sisters stare at him in fright. Still whooping, Jimmy jumped from the chair and ran out of the room. Behind him he heard his mother laughing, delighted with her only son's delight, glad after this tiresome week to have her son back again.

PART TWO: THE CITY SURPRISED

7

EASTER MONDAY

IT WAS MORE THAN A WEEK LATER. It was, to be exact, just before noon on Easter Monday. And in all Dublin – in all the world, maybe – there was no more miserable creature than Jimmy Conway.

He walked in Sackville Street with heavy steps like a man on his way to jail. In *Sackville Street*: that is to say, in Dublin city, and not in Fairyhouse. The impossible had happened: Mick had let him down. His uncle had ruined his life.

Mick had called around on Friday evening, looking very upset. When Jimmy smiled at him he looked even worse. He took Ma aside and whispered to her. She became very angry.

'Oh no you don't,' she hissed out loud to Mick. 'You can tell him yourself.'

Something in her voice chilled Jimmy's heart. When he looked at Mick's face his expression told Jimmy that something terrible had happened. And there was only one thing that it could be, and it was a thing that Jimmy didn't even want to think about.

'Jim, lad,' Mick stammered. 'Jimmy, I ...'

But Jimmy was already shaking his head, willing this new problem to go away. Mick wasn't going to Fairyhouse. Something very important had come up. He was very sorry. He knew, he said, how Jimmy must feel.

'Do you, though?' asked Ma. Jimmy had never heard her sound so angry. 'Do you really understand how high you had that child's hopes? What can be so important, Mick?'

But Mick, who looked almost as upset as Jimmy felt, just shook his head. 'I can't talk about it,' he said.

The ice in Ma's voice changed to fire. 'Is this some political nonsense?' she demanded.

Mick said nothing, but his silence seemed only to confirm her suspicions.

'Mick,' she said, 'you're worse than mad – you're cruel. What good has any of that rubbish ever brought anyone? And now look at Jimmy! You've destroyed that boy.'

Jimmy just stood there. He could feel himself start to shake. Surely Mick wouldn't let him down because of the union or the Citizen Army? Mick had no faith in causes any more; he'd said so himself.

Mick looked helplessly from his sister to his nephew. 'I'm sorry,' he said. He was almost crying. 'I can't say anything more now.'

He turned around suddenly and walked out. Ma followed him to the door and called angrily down the shabby hallway after him: 'May God forgive you, Mick Healy, for destroying a young boy's hopes. May God forgive you, because I don't think Jimmy will be able to. I know I won't.'

Jimmy was too shattered even to cry. It wasn't just missing the races, terrible though that was. But he'd spent days telling everyone about it. All the boys had been impressed and humbled. Older boys, who'd normally not bother talking to a kid like Jimmy, had come to ask him respectfully if the story was true. For a week he'd been the hero of the neighbourhood. And what would everyone think of him now? They'd think he was a liar.

Jimmy spent the rest of the weekend hiding at home, sitting in his mother's chair and staring into the empty fireplace. He couldn't even play his thinking game. If he looked at the face of the old clock now all he saw in his mind was the faces of other boys jeering at him, calling him a braggart and a liar.

By the weekend even Ma's sympathy had started to turn to annoyance. Sarah had got sick on Saturday. She had a fever, and there was no money for a doctor. Ma sat up with her till late on Saturday night and then all night on Sunday, when the fever was at its worst. This morning Ma was exhausted, and the sight of Jimmy sitting there whitefaced, healthy and grieving in the chair was too much for her tired nerves.

'I can't look at you there any more with that long face

on you,' she said, her voice cracking. 'Go out and play. Go out and let me get some peace.'

If she'd sounded angry he might have pleaded or cried, but her voice just sounded more tired and sad than Jimmy could ever remember. It frightened him. He took his cap and went out.

At first he thought he would run away and hide, but that was pointless. He couldn't hide forever. His friends would think he was at Fairyhouse now. Sooner or later someone would see him, and then it would all come out. He'd be revealed as a boaster and a liar. He'd never again be able to hold up his head in their company. His life was ruined, and there was no way of avoiding it.

So Jimmy, for more than an hour now, had been walking in Sackville Street waiting for the inevitable. As time passed, and he met nobody he knew, he started almost to wish that the inevitable would hurry up and arrive. Even the jeering, when it came, could be no worse than this waiting.

Normally on a Monday Sackville Street would be full of passing traffic: carts and carriages, horsemen and motor cars, cyclists and lorries. But this was Easter Monday and today it was drab and half empty, and few fashionable people were to be seen. They had better ways to spend the holiday.

It was a fine spring morning, but Jimmy didn't notice. He was walking blindly, not caring where he was going.

He was heading down the street past Nelson's Pillar when he almost bumped into a small knot of people who had stopped short in front of him.

'There they are,' sneered a haggard old woman in a black shawl. 'The great heroes! The Kaiser's friends!' Her voice dripped with sarcasm.

Jimmy stood at the corner of Henry Street, just beyond the Post Office. Following the old woman's glare, he saw them coming out of Abbey Street – Volunteers, lots of them. And the Citizen Army men were with them! Was that why Mick had betrayed him, for a stupid march? Surely it couldn't be true. You couldn't give up Fairyhouse for a march with a let-on army!

As he too glared at the oncoming men, Jimmy became aware of a strange air about this particular parade. There were a lot of men marching, Volunteers and Citizen Army men together. Behind them trundled an odd collection of slow-moving vehicles – Jimmy noticed a cab, some carts, and a sporty-looking motor car. Men and vehicles were heavily loaded with guns and other equipment. Other traffic paused to let the procession pass as it swung out into Sackville Street.

It was the three men leading the procession who drew Jimmy's eyes. Although they walked just in front of the main body, something set them apart. It was as if they were walking in a world of their own, as blind to the real world around them as Jimmy had been.

He knew two of the men by sight. In the middle was James Connolly, the trade unionist. The headquarters of his union were down by the river in Liberty Hall, quite close to Jimmy's house. Everyone in the slums knew Connolly. His fight for workers' rights had made him a hero to many of the poor. He walked along now in the dark green uniform of the Citizen Army, his thick moustache bristling.

On either side of Connolly strode two men in the lighter green uniform of the Volunteers. One of them was a tall, thin young man wearing glasses. Around his throat was what looked like a bandage. The man looked unwell. He was almost staggering as he marched up the street, but Jimmy was struck by the look of pride and triumph on his pale, haughty face.

The third man Jimmy recognised as Mr Pearse, a schoolteacher who often addressed political meetings. He would speak fiercely about violence and bloodshed and death, and many people regarded him as the greatest lunatic of all the so-called Sinn Féiners – a would-be hero who in his school out in Rathfarnham taught middle-class boys to worship bloodshed and mythical heroes from Ireland's savage past. Yet his face too, like Connolly's, like the face of the sickly young man beside them, was odd now, set in grave lines yet somehow peaceful and happy. It was almost as though the three men were surrounded by a light that came from inside them, that had nothing to do with the real Dublin that they were walking through.

It was unusual to see Connolly and his Citizen Army marching with Pearse and the Volunteers. The two groups didn't really get on. Jimmy looked beyond the three men, at the column still emerging from Abbey Street. They must all be coming from Liberty Hall. Jimmy searched the faces, looking for Mick. There was no sign of him.

The last of the men turned into Sackville Street now, but still Mick wasn't among them. Then, at the very end, came two men with no uniforms. One was a handsome man leaning heavily on a stick, limping. Beside him was an old man with grey, receding hair and a big moustache. Wasn't that the old man who kept the tobacco shop at the top of Sackville Street – Mr Clarke?

What odd people the Sinn Féin leaders were: old Clarke, then the crippled man, the sick-looking young man with the bandaged throat, and Pearse with his fixed stare, and then Connolly like a stocky little bulldog with bandy legs. Yet today they looked different. They looked – yes, that was it – they looked like soldiers, real soldiers, going out to fight for a cause.

Behind the marching men now Jimmy saw some boys of his own age trailing along, laughing and shouting. Jeering the men, Jimmy knew, though this time the marchers were ignoring them completely. The people around him too were making comments.

'Where are they off to now, I wonder?' said the old woman in the shawl.

'They look like they're going camping,' laughed a man in a bowler hat. 'Maybe they're off to visit their friends in Germany, to collect their wages.'

Some people said that the Volunteers were paid by the Kaiser, though Jimmy had never believed it. He'd heard that the Kaiser was mad and evil, but he couldn't believe he would be foolish enough to pay good money to groups like the Volunteers.

Jimmy was looking at the boys who were following the march. He recognised some of his friends. They'd soon pass the place where he stood. It was the moment he'd been dreading, and now it was here he was afraid. Should he turn and run down Henry Street? But something kept him standing there, something that had nothing to do with shame or fear. His eyes moved from the boys back to the marchers, and especially to the three men who led them.

The three leaders came level with the General Post Office, only a few yards from Jimmy. As he watched, Connolly called the column to a halt behind them. The men stopped untidily, some of them bumping into each other. Someone tittered. Then the street seemed to grow suddenly still. Jimmy heard an Angelus bell ringing, and mutterings around him, but his attention was fixed on Connolly.

The trade union man drew himself up to his full height. His face was flushed, but still it wore that air of certainty. He looked, Jimmy thought, as if his own inevitable moment had come. But what was going to happen? A speech? A demonstration?

Connolly shouted. Jimmy felt his mouth drop open as Connolly's words reached his ears.

'Left turn!' Connolly was saying. 'To the GPO – *charge*!'

For a moment even the Volunteers seemed stunned. Then someone else shouted: 'Take the GPO!'

Wild yells broke from the column. The men raced in a ragged charge for the doors of the Post Office.

'Lord save us!' said the old woman. Her voice sounded dry and frightened. 'What do the bowseys think they're doin'?'

Nobody answered her. The other onlookers were as shocked as she was herself.

8

GLORIOUS MADNESS

JIMMY FELT AS THOUGH a storm had broken out inside him on this sunny day. It was a storm of emotions. He knew now that it really was political business that had kept Mick from going to Fairyhouse.

These men who'd just led the attack on the Post Office were then the real cause of Jimmy's shame. He should hate them. But what he actually felt was curiosity and a kind of wonder.

Groups of people were gathering and they chatted excitedly.

'I saw another gang of them going down Grafton Street towards Stephen's Green,' Jimmy heard someone say.

'Volunteers or that union crowd?' someone else asked.

'How do I know?' said the first man. 'They all look the same to me.'

Someone else said there'd been an explosion of some kind in the Phoenix Park, while others told of meeting groups of armed Sinn Féiners at various points around the city. Could the war be coming to Dublin?

Someone touched Jimmy's arm, and he looked around to see the excited face of Tommy Doyle. This was the meeting he'd been most dreading, but Tommy didn't even mention the races. He seemed to have forgotten all about them. He was too interested in Sackville Street now. His face shone with the excitement.

'Did you see them?' he gasped. 'Charging the Post Office!'

'Yeh!' Jimmy said. 'Wasn't it grand?'

Tommy nodded. 'Like the war,' he said. A strange, admiring look came into his eyes as he looked at Jimmy. 'You're a cute one,' he said.

Jimmy was taken aback. 'Me?' he asked. 'Why?'

Tommy gave him a playful dig in the arm. 'It's okay,' he said. 'You kept Mick's secret, but you've no need to let on any more. I wish you'd'a told me – but I suppose it was a military secret.'

Mick's secret? What was all that about? 'Did you see Mick?' Jimmy asked. 'Was he with the Volunteers?'

Tommy grinned. 'I went over to Kevin Street with Billy Moran,' he said. 'He's gone to stay with his sister down there. When I was coming back I saw Mick marching down Grafton Street with the Citizen Army men. I hear they're after taking the Green – but I'm sure you know all about that already. When did Mick tell you?'

Jimmy suddenly understood what Tommy was talking about. Tommy thought the whole Fairyhouse story was some kind of scheme to hide Mick's part in the rebellion – for that's what it must be, a rebellion. Jimmy didn't know what to say. Should he tell the truth?

But Tommy was already leaving. 'I'm going home to tell me Ma,' he shouted back to Jimmy. 'She'll want to see this. See ya later!'

A crash of glass made Jimmy look back towards the Post Office. Men were breaking out the windows there with rifle butts. Pieces of glass were falling down into the street. A woman screamed somewhere, and people began to move off the pavement beneath the rain of shards. A stream of complaining customers was being ejected from the building at the same time. Outside, the onlookers murmured in shock. Most of them didn't yet seem to grasp what was going on.

A rebellion! Jimmy knew there'd been rebellions against England in the past, but he'd never expected to see one himself. That old man who'd been with the Volunteers today, Mr Clarke: people said he was an old revolutionary, one of the ones who'd taken part in the last uprising – but that must be forty or fifty years ago.

Jimmy was excited. So Mick was with the Citizen Army, down in the Green. He found himself wishing he could be down there at Mick's side. He pictured himself with a gun in his hand. The picture surprised him. It was only a week since soldiering had lost all its glamour for him.

People around him were speaking of the Sinn Féiners' madness. It was certainly mad, Jimmy agreed, but it was glorious too, and it thrilled him and heated his blood. The

Volunteers and the Citizen Army were fighting – not for Britain, not for the empire, but for Ireland.

Then Jimmy stopped. *Who* would they be fighting? The British army. There was no-one else here to fight. But his own Da was in the British army, as were thousands of other Irishmen. Many of the soldiers posted in Dublin were Irish – you heard it when they spoke. So, would Irishmen be shooting at each other at home here in Dublin?

Thinking of Da made Jimmy suddenly remember Ma. She would be home now with the girls. And she had no money. This afternoon, though, she'd be coming down to the Post Office along with other soldiers' wives to collect her separation allowance. But with a rebellion going on and the Post Office in the hands of the rebels there'd be no money paid out here today.

'Where the hell are the police?' squawked the old woman beside him. 'They'll soon clear these thugs out!'

Jimmy doubted that very much. He'd seen two policemen quietly slipping away only minutes before, not wanting to get involved. He thought of the look he'd seen on the faces of the Volunteers' leaders. They wouldn't be cleared out by any police force. There would be shooting here. Ma mustn't come here today. He must warn her.

Jimmy took a last look at the Post Office. Men were piling things in the frames of the broken windows, fortifying them. On the street, the crowd was getting bigger. Even Jimmy knew that he was watching history being made. Whatever happened today, one day people would wish that they'd been here to see it. It was also, of course, the most exciting thing that Jimmy had ever seen, and he didn't want to miss a minute of it. But Ma had nobody else to depend on; he could come back later.

Jimmy tore his eyes away from the scene and ran across the street, not looking back. As he ran, he heard the old woman in the shawl shouting a curse at the men who were fortifying the windows.

Once away from Sackville Street everything was completely normal. The scene at the Post Office might have been something from a dream. Jimmy didn't stop running even when he reached his own house. He raced in the front door and up the rotting stairs, jumping over the piles of dirt and rubbish on the landings. He didn't stop until he stood gasping, staring at Ma, trying to get his breath back so that he could tell her the news.

Ma was sitting by the bed where Sarah lay. Sarah was red-faced and moaning, his mother pale and grim. Son and mother looked at each other.

'Ma!' Jimmy got the word out at last. 'Mick ...'

'I know, son,' she broke in. 'He was here just after you went out. He came to explain. He said he couldn't tell us before.'

There was a whimper from the bed beside her, and both of them looked at Sarah. Her face was wet with sweat.

'How is she?' Jimmy asked.

'Worse. She's burning with fever. I sent Josie to Kitty Doyle – I was afraid she'd catch it too.' Ma stood up, wiping her hands on her skirt. She came and stood in front of Jimmy, looking him in the eye. She was pale and tired and worried. 'Jimmy,' she said, 'I think we're in trouble.'

'The Post Office ...' he said. 'The Volunteers are after taking it over. There won't be any money today.'

His mother nodded. Tears came into her eyes. 'It's not just the allowance,' she said. 'It's Ella.'

Jimmy looked at her in surprise: surely she wasn't fretting about Ella *now*. Didn't she have enough problems of her own with a sick child and no money?

Ma seemed to read his thoughts, and shook her head. 'No,' she said, 'it's not what you think. Ella ... Ella made a mistake.' The tears in her eyes overflowed, and she rubbed at them almost angrily. She didn't seem to know what to say. That wasn't like her. Then she began to talk in a low, serious voice. Jimmy knew Ma's serious voice: it meant that something was very wrong.

'Jimmy,' she said, 'Mick didn't think he'd get a chance to get here this morning. He was only here for a minute as it was. When he heard they were going to take over the Post Office, he knew we wouldn't get any money today. So he decided to give us some money of his own – all his savings. It was four pounds, Jimmy. He tried to get over here last night to warn us. He wanted to give us the four pounds, so that we could get some food and get a doctor for Sarah. But he couldn't get away – he was moving supplies to Liberty Hall all day yesterday.'

Four pounds! Jimmy wondered how Mick had saved so much money. Was everything all right after all? But Ma went on before he could ask.

'Mick met Ella in the street,' Ma said. 'He warned her what was going to happen. He told her that he had to get the money to us. She said she'd bring it over this morning. She promised, Jimmy, she promised ... Mick gave her the money, but ...'

'She never came,' said Jimmy. 'She knew Sarah was sick, and she never brought the money! She kept it for herself!'

'Hush!' Ma said, looking nervously over at Sarah. 'We don't know that, Jimmy. Anything might have happened to her. Mick said he'll try and see Ella today to find out what happened. Maybe she's just delayed.'

'But Mick is with the Citizen Army men down in Stephen's Green,' Jimmy pointed out. 'He'll never get a chance to see her.'

Ma gripped his hand tightly. There were tears in her eyes again. 'Maybe not,' she said. 'I said I'd go down to the Green if the fighting didn't start. But I'm afraid to leave Sarah here on her own. Will you stay with her?'

Jimmy's fury faded. Suddenly Ella seemed very unimportant. 'Will Sarah die?' he asked.

His mother finally burst into tears. She hugged him close to her and cried. 'Oh Jimmy,' she said. 'I'm so afraid she will. I've never seen any of you so sick, and I don't know what it is.'

'Then you can't go,' Jimmy said. 'If Sarah gets worse I won't know what to do. I'll go and look for Mick. Nobody will notice me.'

'No! I'd be terrified that something might happen to you out in the streets. If fighting starts ...'

'And what if you go?' Jimmy interrupted. 'What if you go, and something happens to you? Where will we be then?'

It was true, Lily Conway realised. It would have to be him. There was nobody else left. She looked at her son with a new respect.

'You're right, son,' she said. 'But you have to promise me you'll come back straight after. See Mick, ask him about Ella, then come back. Promise me that.'

Jimmy nodded. 'I promise,' he said.

'Promise faithfully,' she said. 'Cross your heart.'

Jimmy crossed his heart and repeated his promise. Ma stood up and dried her eyes. She suddenly became businesslike, as if to distract her mind from worry.

'It might take a while for you to get down to the Green,' she said. 'I have a little bread left. I'll make you some tea. It might be all you'll get for a while.'

Jimmy wanted to protest. He wanted to start out straight

away. But he knew she was right. As she bustled around getting the food ready, Jimmy sat in her chair and looked up at the old clock. But he wasn't playing the thinking game: daydreams were unnecessary when the very stuff of dreams seemed to be spilling out onto the streets around him.

9

TO THE GREEN

BY THE TIME JIMMY HAD FINISHED THE TEA AND BREAD and got out in the streets again it was after one o'clock. He went quickly down Abbey Street, dying to see what had happened. There was no sound of shooting nearby, and there were still people hanging around. They stood in groups, discussing the day's shocking events.

At the corner of Sackville Street he looked up towards the Post Office. In front of the building a tram had been overturned and lay there like the aftermath of some ignored accident.

The Post Office itself seemed quiet. But a group of Volunteers stood outside on the corner of Prince's Street, and there were others up on the roof of the building. There were unfamiliar flags flying from the two flagpoles on the roof. One was green with something written on it,

66

but it was too far away for Jimmy to make out the words. The other was a tricolour of green, white and orange. Jimmy wondered whether that was the German flag.

'The Lancers! The Lancers are coming!' The shout came from behind him. Jimmy looked around. The Volunteers who'd been standing outside the Post Office disappeared into Prince's Street. Other people scattered too. Then, looking up towards the Parnell Monument, Jimmy saw them: a detachment of the British cavalry, their horses prancing as they advanced. Even as he watched they fanned out across the roadway and halted just beyond Nelson's Pillar.

Someone tugged at Jimmy's arm. He turned his head. It was the old woman in the shawl whom he'd last heard calling for the police.

'Get off of the street now, son,' she said. 'The Lancers'll take care of them buckos.'

Jimmy was about to answer her crossly when it struck him that she was right. He followed the old woman into the shelter of a shop doorway. She cowered back in its depths, but Jimmy couldn't resist the urge to peer out.

The officer in charge of the Lancers was holding up his sword. They were going to charge – and with lances! Jimmy couldn't believe it: lances were best kept for daydreams, where enemy guns weren't real.

The Lancers charged. It was a fearsome sight and Jimmy ducked back into the doorway. For a few seconds the air was full of the sound of horses' hooves on the cobbles. Then Jimmy jumped as a ragged, jolting crash of gunfire broke out.

The sound of the hooves faltered. Another booming volley was heard. The hoofbeats thundered again – going away. The Lancers were retreating! Jimmy couldn't help himself: he peeped out cautiously.

His view was partly blocked by the overturned tram, but he saw men and horses lying on the ground in Sackville Street. A Lancer on foot was running up the path near Henry Street, and the main body of cavalry was galloping back towards the Parnell Monument.

The idea that the army might retreat had never actually occurred to Jimmy before. He gaped at the fallen soldiers. There were four of them, and only one seemed to be moving. Two horses lay stretched out beside them. A thick cloud of gunsmoke hung in front of the Post Office.

Without stopping to think, Jimmy ran towards the soldiers on the ground. When he came to the first of the fallen horses, he reached out and pulled the dead Lancer's carbine from its holster in front of the saddle. It was as if someone else was making him move.

The gun was short and light, but it felt heavy in Jimmy's hands. His eyes fell on the dead Lancer lying just beside the horse. He was a young man, lying on his back with his arms flung wide. His eyes and mouth were open, and there was a dark stain on his chest. He had a look of surprise on his dead face.

Someone grabbed at Jimmy's arm. It was the old woman in the shawl.

'What d'ye think ye're doing?' she demanded. She grabbed at the gun, trying to pull it from him. 'Put it back,' she cried, 'ye dirty little rebel!'

For a few seconds they struggled. The woman wasn't much bigger than Jimmy, and she wasn't strong. Terrified, he pushed her. She fell with a shriek. Jimmy didn't stop to see her land; carrying the carbine, he ran towards the Post Office.

'Hey!' he called, holding the gun up towards the nearest of the barricaded windows. 'Here's a gun!'

He had to stand on tiptoe to reach up. A hand appeared and took the other end of the carbine. Jimmy let it go, and the gun disappeared in through the window.

'Thanks, young fella,' called a cheerful voice. 'Good work!'

But Jimmy was already off and running down the street, followed by the blistering curses of the old woman. He didn't stop running till he reached the river. On O'Connell Bridge he had to pause to catch his breath. He leaned against the stone balustrade and gulped in air.

Jimmy was shocked by the enormity of what he'd just done. Not long ago the Lancers had represented all he most admired. It was as if Jimmy were turning his back on the world of dreams. Now he was a rebel too – just as the old woman said. But this wasn't the time to sort these things out. He could think about it later. First he had to find Mick.

His journey to Stephen's Green was peculiar, because most of what he passed seemed so normal and ordinary. People seemed to be going about their everyday business. The streets were fairly empty, but then it was a holiday. As he passed the front of Trinity College, Jimmy heard shooting from Dame Street, but when he looked he saw no sign of anything odd there.

He passed down Grafton Street, narrow and lined with expensive shops. At the far end he came upon a large crowd. Jimmy wormed his way through to the front of the group. Tommy Doyle was right: the Citizen Army *had* taken over the Green.

It was impossible to say how many of them there were, but through the railings Jimmy could see the uniformed men moving around inside the park. There were a lot of them on the streets around the Green too, stopping traffic and making barricades. On the path outside the main gate Jimmy saw a group of uniformed men. Among them he recognised Mick's friend Michael Mallin, dressed in the uniform of a Citizen Army officer.

Mallin was talking to a woman who was also in uniform. She wore boots and trousers, and a big hat with dark feathers in its crown. Jimmy knew her, too. She was the Countess Markievicz, who'd been associated with the trade union during the big strike. She was carrying a gun, and Jimmy thought she looked amazingly glamorous.

A motor car came out of South King Street, near where Jimmy stood. There was a shout, and three rebels ran over and halted it at gunpoint. Two of them carried rifles with fixed bayonets, the third a big revolver. They made the passengers get down from the car, then the man with the revolver got in and forced the driver to turn the vehicle around and drive it into place in a barricade being made further down the street. But Jimmy ignored the car's progress: he'd recognised one of the two riflemen.

'Mr Smith!' he called out. 'Mr Smith!'

Smith was a friend of Da's. Jimmy didn't know him well, but the man always had a cheery hello for him when they passed in the street. Smith had been in the army and had spent time in America, and now he was some kind of reporter. At the moment he looked fierce and impressive in the dark green uniform of the Citizen Army. He smiled when he saw Jimmy.

'Young Conway!' he said. 'Have you come to join up?'

'I'm looking for my uncle Mick,' Jimmy said. 'Did you see him?'

Smith nodded. He pointed in the direction that the car had gone. 'The last time I saw Mick Healy,' he said, 'he was down there by Cuffe Street with Frank Robbins. Have you come from Sackville Street?'

'Yeh,' said Jimmy. 'The Lancers attacked the Post Office

71

but the Volunteers shot them out of their saddles.'

Smith's grin grew wider. He looked positively bloodthirsty. 'Well, isn't that good news, now?' he said. He shouted over to another man. 'Hey, Pat! Did you hear? The cavalry charged the Post Office and were pasted.'

The other man just laughed, thinking it was a joke. Looking at him, Jimmy recognised Paddy Doyle, also in the Citizen Army uniform. Paddy had been due to go for army training this week. It looked as though he'd be getting tougher training than he'd bargained for, though to Jimmy he looked very happy.

'You'd best go find Mick,' Smith said kindly. 'You know, boy, your father will be sorry he missed this.'

Jimmy said goodbye and trotted on, past serious men carrying guns. At the corner of the Green he saw Mick. Like many of the Citizen Army men, Mick had no uniform, but he was carrying a rifle. Jimmy called out to him.

Mick turned. 'Jimmy!' he said. 'What are you doing here? It's dangerous – they might attack us any time.'

'There's not a soldier or policeman between here and the Parnell Monument,' Jimmy said, 'except the Lancers that the Volunteers in the Post Office shot.'

Mick's eyes grew wide at the news. 'You saw that?'

'I saw it. There were four Lancers shot, and two horses. I took a Lancer's gun and gave it to the Volunteers. Was that the right thing to do, Mick?' Jimmy wanted someone to tell him that it was.

Mick looked at him oddly. 'I suppose so,' he said finally. 'But it was very dangerous too. Stay away from any fighting, Jimmy, and don't touch any guns. You might get yourself shot. The best thing you can do is stay home and mind your mother.'

'But Ma sent me here, Mick, to ask you about Ella.'

Mick's face changed. It became closed and angry. 'She never turned up, then?' he asked.

'No. Ma says Ella made a mistake, but ... I don't believe it. I think she kept the money on purpose.'

Mick just sighed. 'I don't know,' he said. 'She knew how important the money was.' He looked at Jimmy. 'It's not really badness, you know,' he continued. 'Ella's just cowardly and easily bullied.'

Jimmy had his own ideas about Ella, things he'd put together from overheard snatches of conversation between her and his Ma. 'Is it Charlie who bullies her?' he asked. 'Because he drinks?'

Mick gave him another odd look. 'Yes,' he said. 'Yes, it is.' He thought for a moment. 'Jimmy,' he said, 'it's no good. I won't be able to go and see Ella. I can't leave my post.'

Jimmy had expected as much. Mick had his duty to do. 'Then I'll have to do it,' he said. 'I'll go to her house.'

Mick looked surprised at the determination in his nephew's voice, but he shook his head. 'That's no good either,' he said. 'Too dangerous. She lives too close to the barracks.'

Ella lived in Northumberland Road, just around the corner from Beggar's Bush barracks. The rebels would be attacking the army barracks there.

Mick was looking thoughtfully at Jimmy. 'Jimmy,' he said, 'you'd better go home. Things could get really rough.'

Jimmy recalled the promises his Ma had made him give. She'd made him cross his heart and swear to come back. You couldn't break a promise when you'd crossed your heart making it. 'Yeah,' he said miserably. 'I'd better go.'

He looked at his uncle. Despite the rifle in his hands and his serious face, Mick looked as boyish as ever. Jimmy wished that he himself was old enough to pick up a gun and fight beside him. Some of the Citizen Army men he'd seen had looked only a few years older than himself.

'Look, Jimmy,' Mick said. 'About Fairyhouse ... I'd never have promised if I'd known about this.'

Impulsively, Jimmy reached out and touched his uncle's arm. 'It's all right, Mick,' he said. 'I understand – now.'

It was true, too: he did understand. Until Mick mentioned it, in fact, he'd completely forgotten about the races. It was hard to believe it had seemed so important only a couple of hours ago.

Mick fumbled in the canvas bag that hung at his belt and pulled out a small parcel wrapped in brown paper. 'Does your Ma have any food in the house?' he asked.

'Tea,' Jimmy said. 'Tea and a bit of bread.'

Mick held out the package. 'Sandwiches,' he said. 'It's all I have.'

'Won't you need them yourself?'

Mick nodded towards a building across the street. 'There's food for us in there,' he said. 'The Countess fixed it up. I just wish I could get some of that for you as well.'

'No,' Jimmy said. 'That's for the fighting men. Mick?' Mick looked at him. 'I'm glad you found your cause again,' Jimmy said. 'Really.'

Mick laid a hand on Jimmy's shoulder. 'You're a good kid, Jimmy,' he said. 'Look after your Ma and your sisters now. You're all they have.'

It was only as he started back up Grafton Street that it hit Jimmy: Mick talked as if he didn't expect to come out of this alive.

10

THE HORDE

WHEN JIMMY REACHED SACKVILLE STREET AGAIN he saw that crowds were gathering. People stood and watched the Post Office as though the building itself were going to do something. They looked like people at a pantomime or a play. Many cursed the Volunteers, but they did it quietly, in worried voices. There were no soldiers or policemen to be seen. Even the dead Lancers had been taken away. Only the Volunteers were on the street in uniform, coming and going on mysterious errands or making barricades on sidestreets.

Jimmy saw a large group of people standing at Nelson's Pillar looking at a notice that was posted there. He hesitated, then went over to see what it was. He pushed to the front of the crowd and looked; it was a poster the rebels had put up.

At the top were some words in Irish. Beneath them was written, in large letters: THE PROVISIONAL GOVERNMENT OF THE IRISH REPUBLIC – TO THE PEOPLE OF IRELAND. Jimmy didn't know what 'provisional' meant, and many of the words that followed were strange too.

'What does it mean?' he asked a man with a moustache.

The man looked down at him haughtily and answered with an English accent.

'It means nothing at all,' he said, 'except that you're all mad here.'

Another man told Jimmy that the Volunteers had declared Ireland an independent country – a republic, whatever that was.

At the bottom of the declaration were the names of the new government's members; among them was Thomas Clarke, the old shopkeeper. Mr Pearse and Mr Connolly's names were there too.

When Jimmy finally reached home little had changed.

Sarah was delirious, burning with fever and Ma looked even more exhausted; she'd been awake now for the better part of two days and two nights. She took Jimmy's bad news well, almost as though she'd expected it. When he gave her Mick's parcel she held it in her hand, looking at it, and said nothing.

Jimmy was going to suggest that he should now go over to Ella's to try and get the money, but something told him not to mention the idea. He was sure Ma would forbid it, and if she did then he'd have to obey her. If he didn't mention the subject he could always go later if he had to. And there was always the chance – a small chance – that Ella had just been delayed. Jimmy didn't believe it, but it was only fair to wait. Everyone deserved a chance.

Meanwhile there was not much he could do to help Ma except to stay out of her way. She'd arranged that Josie should stay up in Doyles' for a couple of days. It would be terrible if she caught the fever too. As for Jimmy, he would just have to take his chances. He wouldn't leave Ma to cope alone. When he told her this, she hugged him.

'God bless you, son,' she said.

Jimmy spent the rest of the morning prowling the room like a caged animal. He was bursting with curiosity, but Ma wouldn't let him out again.

'You can go out later,' she said, 'if it stays quiet.'

In the afternoon Sarah seemed to sleep naturally. Her breathing got quieter. Ma let Jimmy persuade her to lie down too. 'I'll call you if anything happens,' he assured her.

Ma was asleep almost as soon as she lay down. Jimmy made himself sit quietly in her chair, though it was torture for him. He kept imagining what might be happening in Sackville Street.

It was late afternoon when Ma woke. She looked over at Sarah. 'Any change?' she asked.

'She snored a bit,' said Jimmy. 'But that's all.'

There was a knock on the door. It was Tommy Doyle. He was wild with excitement. 'Hello, Mrs Conway,' he shouted. 'It's a great day for Ireland!'

'Do you think so, Tommy?' asked Ma. 'Is your Ma all right? I hope our Josie's not giving her any trouble.'

'I don't think so,' said Tommy. 'I was out all day watching the Rising.'

While I've been sitting here, thought Jimmy.

'Were you in Sackville Street?' Ma asked.

'I just came from there now, to see is Jimmy coming out.'

'What's that noise I hear?' asked Ma. 'It sounds like it's coming from there.'

Jimmy had been hearing noises for some time, a growling sound like a lot of voices together. It wasn't the sound of fighting, but a strange seething sound he'd never heard before.

'It's only people,' said Tommy. 'Sackville Street is packed.'

This was too much for Jimmy.

'Please, Ma, can I go and look?' he pleaded. 'It can't be dangerous.'

Ma thought for a minute. 'Oh, all right,' she said at last. 'But come back at the first sign of trouble.'

Jimmy raced down the stairs. Tommy could hardly keep up with him.

'What's it like?' Jimmy asked when they got to the street.

Tommy looked at him with a grin. 'It's better nor Christmas!' he said. He reached into his pocket and took out a handful of sweets. 'Here! Have them. I've loads more.'

'Who gave you the money?' Jimmy asked.

Tommy laughed. 'Money?' he said. 'What money?'

Jimmy gaped. 'What are you talking about?'

'Come and see,' Tommy said, and he took off down the street with Jimmy following.

Just before they reached Sackville Street Tommy stopped. He turned to Jimmy, grinning wildly, and threw his sweets in the air. 'Hurray!' he yelled, as the sweets rained down on him.

Jimmy stared. 'Are you gone mad or what?' he asked.

'Ireland is free!' Tommy said. 'And Irish sweets are free too!'

He led Jimmy around the corner. Sackville Street looked as if a herd of elephants had trampled through it. It had been ransacked by a marauding host, out for loot. The host was still there, and it was still looting. This was the source of the strange seething sound. It was the great hungry horde of Dublin's poor.

Wherever Jimmy looked he saw smashed windows: Noblett's and Lemon's sweetshops, Dunn's the hatters, Frewen and Ryan's, the Cable bootshop – everywhere.

The wide street was strewn with abandoned packaging and bits of glass. Jimmy saw dumped hats, boots, underwear, toys and cakes – a huge litter of expensive things. A street paved with luxury goods, like something from a dream. There seemed to be thousands of people moving restlessly through the street in unruly surges. They must have looted the pubs too because a great many of them were very drunk.

'It's great!' shouted Tommy. 'You can take anything you like.'

And that's exactly what people had done. They were wandering around with strange luxury items that would never be of any use to them. Jimmy saw a boy hardly older than himself playing with a set of golf clubs. As each ball arched off down the street he would follow it through a pair of expensive binoculars that were hanging round his neck.

'That's Jimmy Murphy. His Da will kill him if he sees them clubs. He's a mad Gaelic games man,' Tommy said.

Like many people on the street Jimmy Murphy was wearing a new hat. Others wore two or three different hats at the same time, all crammed on top of each other on their heads.

One boy, a few years younger than Jimmy, was helping a woman who might have been his grandmother to carry big piles of clothes. They'd emerge from the crowd, staggering under huge loads and put them down at a spot in the road close to where Jimmy stood. Then they'd go back for another load. Every time they left, other people would wander over and take most of the things from the pile they'd just brought. Then the boy and the old woman would come back with more clothes. They didn't seem to notice that the pile wasn't growing any bigger.

There was an odd fixed look on the faces of most of the looters, almost a crazy look. It was a look that frightened Jimmy. It was as if a kind of madness had come down and struck hundreds of people at the same time.

Beside Jimmy, Tommy was taking fresh handfuls of sweets from his pockets. 'Have some,' he offered.

But Jimmy shook his head. He was so stunned by what he was seeing that he'd almost forgotten Tommy was there.

The dead horses of the Lancers were still lying in the road and a woman was using one of them as a seat. She was young and pretty, but she was drinking from a bottle and was obviously quite drunk. As Jimmy watched, she tried to stand up but fell back down in a flurry of petticoats. She began to sing something, though he couldn't hear her words above the rumble of the crowd. A big man went over and touched the girl's shoulder, and she swung at him drunkenly with the bottle. Then a surge of the crowd hid both of them from Jimmy's view, and instead he watched two other drunken young women fighting.

'Look at them mots!' said Tommy.

The women were both dressed in rags, and they were fighting over a silk dress. Each of them had a grip on one end of it, and was pulling frantically with the gripping hand. At the same time they were both scratching and clawing at each other's faces with the free hand. Their faces were bloody, and the dress they fought over had been torn and dirtied by their struggle. It was hardly better now than the rags that they were already wearing.

Jimmy saw so many strange and terrible things that he couldn't take all of them in. In the crowd he saw people he knew, but they seemed completely changed. Their faces wore a look of awful hunger. It was the look of people who'd never in their lives had anything at all and are suddenly free to have everything they want. It was a look of pure hunger let loose. It frightened and disgusted Jimmy, but he couldn't find it in himself to blame them or feel that they were evil. The real evil, the evil that made it possible for them to have such savage hunger, was the way that they were forced to live in total poverty every day.

But Jimmy wouldn't venture out into Sackville Street; he was afraid that if he went among the crowds their madness would take him over too. He just stood at the corner and watched the incredible scenes.

'Janey mack, Jimmy! You're gettin' to be a right softie!' said Tommy. 'I'm going. Are you coming or not?'

Jimmy shook his head and Tommy was gone in a flash.

Two Volunteers appeared near Jimmy. They'd obviously been trying to control the crowd, and they'd just as obviously failed. They were both in uniform, but instead of guns they carried long wooden clubs like police batons. One of them was a middle-aged man with a thick grey moustache and a hard, grave face. His companion was much younger, maybe Mick's age. At first Jimmy thought that the younger man was hurt, because he was leaning heavily on the older one. Then Jimmy realised that he was crying.

The two stopped close to where Jimmy stood, and he made out the words that the younger one was saying. 'They don't understand,' he sobbed, over and over. 'They don't understand.'

Jimmy understood, though; and he knew what was wrong with the young Volunteer too. The man was disappointed that the crowds were not living up to his ideals. He looked healthy and well fed, as though he came from a comfortable home. He would know nothing about real hunger and want. Jimmy understood the looting. He didn't like it, but he did understand it. It was the Volunteer, he thought, who didn't have a clue.

11

THE CHOICE

WHEN JIMMY GOT HOME, Ma knew at once that he was upset about something. He tried to tell her about the terrible things he'd seen in Sackville Street and about the strange, mad atmosphere. He couldn't explain it properly, but she seemed to understand. She hugged him tightly.

'There's nothing we can do about that, Jimmy,' she said. 'There's nothing we can do about anything now. All we can do is survive and hope.'

Jimmy found himself crying in her arms. Normally he was ashamed of crying, but now the whole world seemed suddenly so strange that he didn't mind. There was nothing normal left anyway. He felt very tired – exhaustion seemed to come from deep inside him. It was as if he'd gone through too many emotions today; he was used up.

Lily Conway felt him slump in her arms. She looked at him carefully, and felt his forehead.

'You must go to bed, Jimmy,' she said. 'You've had a long day. I don't want you getting sick too. Your forehead is hot.'

Reluctantly, Jimmy went to bed, and as soon as he lay down he fell asleep, and spent a restless night dreaming of war. The people in his dreams were all people he knew, but in the dreams they had become sinister and threatening. His sleep was long, but it was not peaceful.

He woke as it was getting light on Tuesday morning. On the big bed in the far corner his Ma slept fully dressed beside Sarah. She must have tried to stay up all night again, but she'd been too tired. Sarah looked pale, but her breathing was easier and she was no longer tossing in her sleep.

It was quiet outside. In the distance now and then Jimmy heard something that might have been shooting. Memories of last night's scenes in Sackville Street came back to him, mixed up with bits of his dreams. Had he really seen all those things? He decided to take a quick look at the streets today, before anyone woke up.

He slipped quietly out of the house. Outside the sky was cloudy, and it looked as though it might rain. On the short journey he saw nobody move. He did, though, pass several people lying in the streets. At first he thought they must be dead, but then he realised that they had got blind drunk on stolen liquor and had passed out in the streets. They were the dregs of last night's marauding crowd.

Sackville Street was desolate. The roadway was covered with a litter of abandoned loot, much of it trampled to pieces by the mob. Now the mob was gone, for the time being at least, but the gutted shops and ruined merchandise were proof that they'd been here. That much at least had been no dream, whatever Jimmy might prefer to believe.

Jimmy turned and started for home, climbing over a pile of loot that someone had abandoned. There were new shoes and clothes, broken boxes, even a big chair from one of the furniture stores. A toy baby-carriage had been filled with bottles of rum and brandy, but it had overturned and the bottles were all smashed. Jimmy eyed the assortment of articles. They looked like the senseless mixture of things that you might see in dreams.

A basket lying at the edge of the pile caught his eye. It was closed, but he had seen baskets like it before; some of the department stores displayed them in their windows. They were picnic baskets, filled with food – tins of cooked meat and biscuits and bottles of wine. Jimmy had seen toffs and army officers carrying them on summer days as they set off for the seaside with their ladies.

Jimmy stood looking down at the basket. He didn't even want to touch it. The looting was a part of the rebellion he didn't want to be involved in. But what if the basket was full of food? Even if Ma did get money, the shops would stay closed because of the fighting. Most of them here were looted anyway. And somebody had already stolen this basket from one of them; if Jimmy didn't take it, it might just be left here to rot.

He took a quick look around him. Apart from a drunken young woman who was sleeping half-dressed in a shop doorway nearby there was no-one around. With a quick, furtive movement Jimmy bent and scooped up the picnic basket by its metal handle. He hurried away with it, blushing.

The basket felt light – it wasn't full. Jimmy stopped and raised one side of the hinged lid and looked inside. He saw a jumble of tin cans. FRUIT PUDDING, said one; another had EXCELLENT PRESSED TONGUE written on it in fancy letters. They weren't foods that Jimmy knew, but at least they were foods. There were only six tins left in the basket; the rest must have fallen out.

Sarah and Ma were still asleep when Jimmy got back to the house. He lit a fire in the grate and put water on to boil. He took the tins from the basket and put them on the table. Then, struck by an idea, he chopped the wicker basket roughly into pieces with the kitchen knife and fed the pieces to the fire. Nobody could accuse him of stealing if there was no evidence. The food, of course, was still here, but not for long.

When the water boiled Jimmy put some tea-leaves into the blackened teapot and poured boiling water over them. Then he put the teapot and the two cracked mugs on the table beside the tins of food. He went over and woke his mother.

'I'm after making tea, Ma,' he said softly in her ear.

Ma started guiltily and sat up. 'I fell asleep!' she said. She turned to check on Sarah.

'How is she?' Jimmy asked.

'Still feverish, but I think it's gone down a bit.'

'Maybe she'd like some tea?'

'Let her sleep,' Ma said. 'I'll give her something later.'

She stood up and rubbed her eyes. She still looked tired. She went over to the table to pour some tea, and then she saw the tins.

'Jimmy!' she said. 'Where did these come from?' Her voice wasn't sharp or suspicious, only surprised. Faltering, Jimmy explained. His face grew red, and he stopped several times during the story. But Ma didn't give out to him when she heard it; instead, she hugged him close. 'Oh, Jimmy!' she said, 'you're a brave lad and a good one.'

'I didn't know what to do,' he said. 'I knew it was wrong to take it, but it was wrong to leave you here with no food too.'

'Hush!' Ma said, hugging him tighter. 'You were brave, Jimmy. Brave and good.' She tried to explain. 'Jimmy,' she said, 'you know it's wrong to shoot at people.'

Jimmy was puzzled. 'Yeh,' he said.

'But your father is in the army, and he shoots at people. And now Mick is out fighting, and maybe he'll have to shoot at people too.'

'But that's different ...' He stopped. It was a complicated matter. He didn't have the words to express himself.

'Sometimes,' his mother said, 'taking things that aren't yours is the same. It's wrong. But you knew it would be more wrong to leave us with no food while this lay thrown away in the street.'

Jimmy saw that she understood. He nodded enthusiastically. Ma stood up, laughing almost gaily. Jimmy knew that she was doing it to reassure him. She made a great show of reading the labels on the cans.

'Excellent pressed tongue, indeed! Maybe we won't be eating much for the next few days, Jimmy,' she said, 'but we'll be eating very fancy stuff.'

'I'll bring one of these tins up to Mrs Doyle,' she went on. 'She has a bit more food than we do, but she has our Josie up there as well as her own.' She examined the tinned food again. 'We're not too badly off at all.' It was a lie, but Jimmy knew that Ma thought keeping his spirits up was more important.

Jimmy, though, wasn't cheered. A few cans of food and a couple of stale sandwiches from Mick wouldn't last long, and there was no way of knowing how long it would be before they would get anything else.

So far the British had made no serious effort to force the Volunteers out of Sackville Street, but that wouldn't last. The army would attack and the rebels would fight. When that happened, Jimmy and his family would be in the middle of a battlefield.

Things couldn't be like this all over the city. He was sure of that. There didn't seem to be a huge number of rebels. They would defend the places they'd taken over, but other parts of Dublin might be calm. Shops might be open and people able to move around in safety.

Jimmy thought about his aunt Ella. He would bet on it that there'd be food in Ella's house. But Mick had warned him not to go there. If the rebels did attack the barracks at Beggar's Bush, then Northumberland Road where Ella lived would indeed be dangerous. But thinking about Ella, about the four pounds that she had kept, made Jimmy angry. It made him so angry that danger didn't seem to matter very much. It would be dangerous here too, when the army finally attacked the Post Office.

There were only two things that could be done, Jimmy thought. Either his family must get away from here, or they must get money or food from Ella. Getting away was impossible: Sarah couldn't be moved. Besides, they'd nowhere to go. With money they might find lodgings in some safer part of the city, but without money it would be hopeless. Certainly there was no question of them going to Ella: Charlie Fox would have no pity on them. Ella would hardly welcome them either – she'd never even asked them to tea.

The only thing to do was to go to Ella's for money or food, and if someone had to go to Ella's, then that someone must be Jimmy. But Ma would never agree. There was only one thing for it. He'd have to deceive her. Nothing could be worse than the position that his family was in now. Anything that helped them had to be right.

Jimmy's mind was made up.

12

THE YOUNG VOLUNTEER

THE FOLLOWING MORNING JIMMY WOKE EARLY. He heard no movement. In the half-light he saw that Ma and Sarah were still asleep, their heads on the same pillow. Sarah had slept through most of yesterday, but had woken for long enough to eat some soup from one of Jimmy's tins. It was the first food she'd had for days, a sign that her fever had lessened.

Jimmy got up quietly now. He heard no sounds outside. He didn't hesitate: he was afraid that if he did he wouldn't go at all. He'd feel too guilty, thinking of Ma's worry. He wished he could leave her a note, but they had no pens or pencils and he couldn't think what he might say.

He crept to the door and turned the handle. It made no noise. As soon as the gap was wide enough he squeezed out through it and closed the door quietly behind him.

It wasn't fully light. The hall and stairs were still dark. There was a drunk asleep on the landing, but Jimmy skipped over him lightly and continued on his way. Outside he saw no-one, just one more huddled form snoring by some railings.

Jimmy looked mistrustfully at the sky. It had rained yesterday evening, and he hoped it wouldn't rain again today. The thin, worn jacket that he was wearing was his only coat. His head felt a bit odd, and he hoped that he hadn't caught Sarah's fever. That would be a disaster.

Sackville Street was deserted. Most of the roadway and pavement were covered with broken and abandoned loot. It made a thick layer that had been soaked by the rain and then trampled underfoot.

'What are you doing here, boy?' The voice came from behind him. Jimmy jumped in fright and whirled around.

A Volunteer carrying a rifle was looking at him from the recess of a shop doorway. The man's face was white, his eyes rimmed with dark circles. He looked exhausted.

'Well?' the Volunteer demanded. 'Are you deaf? I said what are you doing here? Looking for something to steal, is it? You're too late, your mates have already taken it all.' His voice was sour under the tiredness.

'I'm doing nothing,' Jimmy said. He swallowed. 'I just came to see what was happening. I was afraid the British might be here.'

The young Volunteer smiled, but it was a bitter smile. 'They are,' he said. He gestured up Sackville Street with his rifle. 'Look for yourself. They haven't started shooting yet, but they're here all right.'

Jimmy stared up Sackville Street. There were figures moving about near the Parnell Monument at the top of the street. Jimmy could just make out the khaki of their uniforms.

'They came during the night,' the young Volunteer said. 'It's swarming with them up there – and down the other end too, beyond the river. They took our positions around the City Hall.'

'City Hall? I heard there was shooting down that way yesterday.'

'There was plenty of that. I'm sure the Citizen Army gave them a lot to worry about.'

'I've an uncle in the Citizen Army,' Jimmy said. 'He's in the Green.'

The young Volunteer's face softened. 'An uncle, eh?' he said. 'And are you proud of him, boy?'

''Course I am,' Jimmy said without hesitation.

The man nodded in approval. 'The Green is empty now,' he said finally. 'The British brought machine-guns up yesterday. Mallin took the men into the College of Surgeons. There's nobody now in the Green but the dead.'

The dead. The words hit Jimmy like a slap in the face. Was Mick one of those dead in the Green? Was he lying there now, with his arms stretched out like the young Lancer in Sackville Street on Monday?

'I have to get across the river,' he said to the young rebel. 'Would I get over O'Connell Bridge?'

The young man pondered. 'No,' he said. 'The shooting will start in earnest soon. They'll attack today.'

'And ... will they drive you out?' Again Jimmy blushed, aware that his question was two-edged. He did not want the British to drive them out, but if the army did dislodge the rebels from Sackville Street then the fighting would move somewhere else and his family would be safe.

The Volunteer pointed towards the Post Office. 'Look at that place,' he said. 'It's like a fortress. They'd need artillery to get us out – that or a very hard fight.'

He seemed to come to life now. He put the butt of his rifle on the ground, and leaned on the barrel. 'If you have to cross the river,' he said, 'it might be safer down at Tara Street. You can cut down by the quays. Don't go near Amiens Street, though; the British are there too. See what's going on around Liberty Hall. If it's quiet there you'll be grand.'

'But won't the army attack Liberty Hall?'

'They can if they like, but there's nobody there.'

He stretched and yawned. Jimmy wondered if he'd been keeping watch from the doorway all night.

'I must go,' said the Volunteer. He reached into his pocket and felt for something. He held out a slab of chocolate. 'Here,' he said.

Jimmy took the chocolate. He'd had nothing to eat since yesterday. 'Thanks,' he muttered.

The Volunteer walked carefully to the corner and looked up and down Sackville Street. He gave Jimmy a last smile. 'Good luck, son,' he said, and ran out into the street.

Jimmy watched the young man go. He didn't run in a straight line, but zigzagged after every few yards. Jimmy heard several flat cracks that must be rifles. They sounded different from the rebel guns.

None of the bullets hit the young man. He crossed Sackville Street safely and disappeared into Prince's Street.

Jimmy looked again towards O'Connell Bridge, then back up towards the army. He would try Butt Bridge, as the Volunteer had suggested. It was the next bridge downriver. All Jimmy had to do was avoid the larger streets as he worked his way towards it. That would be simple enough; he knew the backstreets and alleyways like the back of his hand.

With a last look at the Post Office, Jimmy went back down Abbey Street. It was time to enter enemy territory.

13

THE BRITISH ARMY

NORMALLY IT WASN'T MUCH MORE than a five-minute walk down Abbey Street to Beresford Place, where the bridge crossed the Liffey between Liberty Hall and the mass of the Customs House. Today, though, it took Jimmy more than twice that long to get there. He went slowly and very carefully, all the time feeling that he was being watched. He couldn't see anybody, but there might be Volunteers in some of the Abbey Street houses. The British were close by as well; maybe they too were sending men into houses, closing in on the rebel positions.

Jimmy didn't like feeling watched, so he took to the backstreets. After a few steps into Old Abbey Street he saw an overcoat lying in the gutter. It was a bit stained from lying in the street, but otherwise it seemed brand new. Maybe someone carrying a bundle of stolen clothes had dropped it without noticing.

It looked as if it had come from the boys' department of some fancy shop. Jimmy took a quick look around him, but saw nobody. He bent and picked up the coat, and quickly put it on. It was too big for him, but fitted better over his jacket. He decided to keep it. He might be away for a long time, and the coat would keep him dry if the rain came again.

Just behind Liberty Hall, Jimmy walked carefully out into Beresford Place. He saw nothing moving on either side of the river. To his left was the great bulk of the Customs House. Ahead was the river itself, the Liffey, crossed here by Butt Bridge and the overhead railway bridge.

The whole area was unnaturally quiet and empty. Jimmy was suddenly afraid, for no good reason that he could see. Maybe it was just the idea of crossing the river. He stepped out into Beresford Place, heading for the bridge.

Movement on the river caught his eye, and he looked down the Liffey. A boat was steaming up towards the bridge. Jimmy quickened his pace. The sooner he got across the river, the better he would feel.

Every step across the bridge seemed to take a very long time. He swung his arms by his sides. He wanted it to be clear to anybody looking that he was just a defenceless boy minding his own business. He had no gun. He wasn't dangerous. There was no reason for anyone to shoot him.

In the still morning air he heard a clatter of metal on stone from behind him. He looked casually over his shoulder, and suddenly noticed men looking out from the roof of the Customs House. They wore military caps and carried rifles. They were the British army and he was walking right under their guns!

'You there!' roared a voice. 'Boy!' For the second time that morning Jimmy's heart skipped a beat. He stopped, uncertain, then looked over to Burgh Quay on the other side of the river, where the call had come from. A man was staring at him. He had a very red face.

'Get off that bridge, quick!' he roared at Jimmy. 'Come on! Get over here!' The man had a Northern Irish accent. There was urgency as well as command in his voice, and Jimmy found himself obeying. He ran towards Burgh Quay, his eyes fixed on the red face.

The man's eyes glared at him. 'Come here!' he ordered. He was a soldier. He reached out and grabbed Jimmy's arm, and flung the boy to the ground.

'What have we here, then?' he growled. 'A little rebel spy, is it?' He was a big man and he wore sergeant's stripes. Two soldiers were with him. The sergeant gripped Jimmy's arm tightly and he gasped with pain.

Fear and pain made Jimmy dumb. He shook his head, helpless. Then came the most frightening sound that he had ever heard in his life. It was a great, roaring boom, as though all the fireworks in the world had gone off at once. It came from close by, and was followed almost immediately by a huge metallic shrieking clang. Jimmy heard himself whimpering in terror. The soldiers, even the sergeant, had flinched too.

One of the younger soldiers looked down the quay,

and someone down there shouted something to him. 'Stupid swine,' said the soldier amiably. 'They hit the railway bridge.'

The sergeant swore. 'Trust the bloody navy,' he said bitterly.

Jimmy felt himself grow suddenly cold inside. It was no longer just fear for himself. He knew now what was going on: the boat on the river was a British Navy boat. The British were shelling Dublin city!

The sergeant pulled Jimmy up until his face was only inches from his own. The sergeant's face was hard and rough, with a scar high on one cheek. His bright blue eyes bored into Jimmy's.

'Well?' he said. 'What's your business here?'

'Please, sir,' said Jimmy. 'My Ma sent me out to look for food. There's none on the northside.'

The sergeant still stared suspiciously into Jimmy's eyes. Jimmy almost whimpered again. This man, now, did look like an enemy.

'Oh, come off it, sergeant,' said one of the other two soldiers. 'He's just a kid. He's no rebel – anyone can see that.' The soldier also had an Ulster accent, but his voice was soft and kindly.

The sergeant grunted thoughtfully. His face relaxed. His grip on Jimmy's arm relaxed a little too. 'You say there's no food up there, eh?' he asked.

'No, sir,' said Jimmy quickly. 'Not a scrap. The shops

were all looted. My sister is sick and my Ma is afraid to go out and leave her.'

'Looting, eh?' said the third soldier. 'Damned rebels!'

Jimmy wanted to shout at the small, thin-faced soldier that it certainly wasn't the rebels who'd been looting, that the Volunteers had actually tried to stop it. But he kept silent, afraid of giving his sympathies away. Help came, though, from an unexpected quarter.

'You ever been in them slums up there, Proctor?' the sergeant asked.

'No, sergeant,' said the thin-faced soldier.

The sergeant grunted in scorn. 'Then, you don't know what you're talking about,' he said. 'They're the filthiest slums in Europe – even worse than the ones you come from, Proctor. It's a disgrace to make people live like that.'

The thin man's face flushed, but he said nothing.

'If there was looting,' the sergeant said, 'then it was them poor people up there that did it – and more power to them, I say. I'm only surprised they never did it before.'

There was another tremendous boom that caught all of them by surprise. It was followed almost immediately by the sound of rending masonry, and by a loud cheer from many voices.

'That sounds a bit better,' said Proctor, who seemed glad to change the subject.

'Please, sergeant,' said Jimmy. 'Where are they shelling? My family is back there.'

The sergeant looked at him, tight-lipped. 'Aye,' he said. 'Well, if the navy can shoot at all then your family should be fine. They're firing at Liberty Hall.'

'But it's empty!' Jimmy exclaimed. His words were drowned out by a rattle of machine-gun fire. The sergeant peered out over the top of the crate he was using for shelter.

'Here, Martin,' he said. 'Get this kid out of here. We can't have children wandering around with a fight about to start.'

Private Martin smiled at Jimmy. 'Right, young fellow,' he said. 'You come with me.'

'Get him a cup of tea or something,' said the sergeant gruffly. 'He looks as if he could do with it.'

Jimmy's efforts to think of these men as enemies were beginning to weaken – enemies didn't give you cups of tea.

Martin beckoned Jimmy to follow him and moved across the road, crouched down and running. Jimmy almost told him not to worry, that there was nobody shooting at him. But the world had turned so strange that he was afraid to tell anyone anything.

14

THE FRIENDLY ENEMY

WHEN HE FOLLOWED THE DODGING SOLDIER into Tara Street Jimmy got yet another shock. There was a mass of khaki figures by the fire station at the bottom of the street. He would have seen them from the bridge if the sergeant hadn't distracted him.

'What's your name, lad?' Martin asked. He was walking upright now that they were out of danger from the imagined guns.

'Jimmy. Jimmy Conway.'

'Good,' Martin said. 'I'm Jimmy too. Jimmy Martin.'

The machine-guns began to fire again from behind them, and were joined by a rattle of rifle fire. From the redbrick tower of the fire station ahead Jimmy saw a flicker of flames. He realised that there was a machine-gun post up there. It seemed strange to spend so much effort when a simple check would show that Liberty Hall was undefended.

'There's loads of soldiers here,' he said.

'Thousands in the city,' Martin told him. 'And fresh troops landed from England last night too. You needn't worry – it will all be over soon. You worried about your people back home?'

'Yes,' Jimmy said. And my people in the Post Office and the Green, he thought, but he kept that to himself.

'It shouldn't be any problem for us,' Martin said.

Jimmy felt he should say something good about the rebels. The confidence of the army seemed almost insulting. He remembered what the young Volunteer in Abbey Street had said.

'The Post Office is built like a fort,' he told Martin.

Behind them the boat's gun boomed again. Martin jerked his head in the direction of the sound.

'Them guns knock down forts,' he said simply.

They were close to the soldiers by the fire station now. The men were relaxing, sitting or standing around at the corner with Brunswick Street. Waiting for the order to attack, Jimmy thought. He hesitated. Martin noticed, and smiled down at him. 'It's all right,' he said. 'They're a rough-looking lot, but it's not you they're after.'

Then they were among the soldiers. Martin asked about getting some tea. After a while someone put a steaming mug in Jimmy's hands. Jimmy felt terrified among these khaki figures. Soldiers were no longer people whose marches you followed: they were people whose job it was to shoot other people. He knew that he would never follow a parade again. Parades were just things that soldiers did in between shooting people. Jimmy tried not to think of his Da.

The tea was hot and sweet and strong and tasted very good. The soldiers were friendly in a gruff way. In between sips from the mug Jimmy tried to answer their questions about how things were beyond the river.

'You say all the people are still in their houses up there?' one of them asked.

'They had no chance to get out.'

'You got out, though,' said another man.

Jimmy explained that he'd had to. He talked again about the lack of food, about his father fighting in France and his sick sister burning with fever. It was a good performance, and the soldiers were sympathetic.

'He's a brave wee fellow,' said a corporal with hair so grey it was almost silver. 'I hope my lad would do the same if this was Belfast.'

'Brave!' said Martin. 'I should say he's brave! Why, you should have seen him coming across that bridge, swinging his arms. Every gun in the place was aimed at him, and he crosses over as cool as you please.'

The men were impressed. There were mutterings of praise all round.

When he had gulped down his tea Jimmy said that he must be going. He invented a relative who lived, he said, in Fitzwilliam Square. But he was almost caught out by one soldier, who obviously knew Dublin fairly well.

'That's a very posh area for you to have a relative in isn't it?' he asked, eyeing Jimmy's clothes. Even the new coat looked shabby after its night in the gutter.

'Oh,' said Jimmy, thinking quickly, 'she's a maid there.'

The soldiers asked him to wait a minute. Jimmy thought he had given the game away.

The corporal with the silver hair went around among the men. When he had finished he came back and gave Jimmy a heavy handful of coins.

'There's nearly five shillings there, lad,' he said. 'If you can't find your relative then you can try to get some food in a shop. Someone will tell you where to find one open.'

Jimmy took the money with a red face and stammered thanks. It was more money than he'd ever held in his hands before – almost a quarter of a guinea! He thrust the pile of coins into the pocket of his soiled new coat. As he did, he felt something else that was in the pocket already. It was something cold and metallic.

The thought struck him that it might be a gun or weapon of some kind. He was too frightened to feel it further, but pulled his hand out of the pocket as though he'd touched something red hot. He must get away and check this.

There were more delays as the soldiers argued among themselves about the best route for him to take. Jimmy listened impatiently. His heart had been pounding since finding the metal thing in his pocket. It didn't feel heavy enough to be a gun, but he hoped that it wasn't a bullet or a knife. If it was then he must get rid of it. It would be fatal if he were searched by any soldiers and found to have a weapon. They would be sure he was a spy, in spite of his age.

Even when he did get away from the soldiers, Jimmy wasn't alone. Private Martin insisted on going with him for a small part of the way.

'You're my responsibility,' he said. 'If our men at Trinity College see you walking with me they'll know you're all right. A true, loyal Dubliner, aren't you?'

Loyal to what though, Jimmy wondered. He didn't dare refuse the offer. Trembling, he thanked the other soldiers for the money. They bade him a cheerful goodbye, their good wishes blending with the boom and crack and rattle of the gunfire around them.

15

FINDING AN UNCLE

AS SOON AS JIMMY MARTIN LEFT HIM, Jimmy felt nervously in his overcoat pocket, trying to identify the metal thing he'd found there. No, it wasn't a knife. It was a narrow rectangle of ...

Jimmy almost laughed when he realised what it was. He pulled it out of his pocket and looked at it – a harmonica, shining in the morning sun. How it had got in the pocket in the first place he could only guess. Looted, like the coat itself, he supposed.

The clock on Trinity College said half-past eight. Through the railings there Jimmy could see khaki figures on guard. From the roof other soldiers, snipers, were firing now and then towards Sackville Street. There was no doubt who was in charge of this part of Dublin, only a few hundred yards from the rebel headquarters.

There were civilians walking in Grafton Street, and Jimmy was tempted to go down there as he had on Monday. If he went right along down Nassau Street now he might reach Ella's house before nine. But he wanted to see the Green again. He wanted to know whether his uncle Mick ... Jimmy made himself finish the thought ... he wanted to know whether Mick was still alive.

Jimmy made up his mind. The soldiers had advised him not to go down Grafton Street or nearby Dawson Street. It stood to reason that their advice would be sensible: soldiers had to be experts at not getting shot.

So Jimmy made for Kildare Street, which would also take him to Stephen's Green, and he turned down there. No-one interfered with him. At the bottom of the street he looked across the road through the railings into the deserted park.

The shooting was right above him now. If he looked up he could see the flashes of the army guns firing from the Shelbourne Hotel. Now and again a spurt of dust was kicked from the hotel walls by rebel bullets answering their fire.

The Green itself looked empty, though it was hard to see much through the screen of trees inside the railings. Then Jimmy noticed two men in Citizen Army uniform lying on the grass. They lay perfectly still, and he knew they were dead. He could not see their faces, but the fact that they wore uniforms meant that neither of them was Mick. That was little comfort: there might be any number of men lying dead in the park, hidden by the trees.

There were quite a few civilians standing around on this corner of the Green. Boys of his own age ran among them, playing. The boys seemed to find it all very exciting. The adults stood looking, quietly discussing the situation.

A machine-gun sounded a brisk rat-tat-tat, like a stick being dragged along railings. The British rifles cracked. The Irish guns made a variety of sounds, the most common a dull, heavy boom that sounded almost like artillery.

A quick movement by the railings of the Green caught Jimmy's eye. One of the boys was squeezing through the railings. Jimmy recognised him – it was Billy Moran, Tommy Doyle's friend. Jimmy remembered Tommy saying that Billy was staying with his sister in nearby Kevin Street.

As Jimmy watched, Billy ran over to one of the dead rebels and picked up the man's pistol. The other boys shouted encouragement.

Jimmy stared, horrified. He thought of Mick's warning about picking up guns. Billy was in full view of the Shelbourne Hotel. He was only playing, of course, but the army wouldn't know that.

Billy Moran stood with the gun in his hand, looking over at his friends in triumph. Jimmy wanted to shout a warning at him. Before he could, the body of the rebel at Billy's feet jerked strangely. It was as if the dead man had come to life. Billy saw the movement and stared down, frightened.

Jimmy realised instantly what had happened: a soldier in the hotel had fired at Billy Moran and missed, hitting the dead rebel instead. Jimmy opened his own mouth to scream at Billy, to tell him to drop the pistol. Before he could say anything Billy Moran seemed to leap in the air, the pistol falling from his hand. He collapsed on the ground and lay still, his bare feet trailing over the dead rebel's back. A woman standing close to Jimmy screamed.

The sight seemed to trigger something in Jimmy; he found himself suddenly running, as if his feet rather than his head had come to a decision.

He crossed the road at the side of the Green furthest from Grafton Street, running as though something was chasing him. It was as though the shot that had killed Billy Moran had acted as a starting pistol in some race that Jimmy was running alone; like a lone horse thundering around the track at his own private Fairyhouse, he was off.

The British army positions lay along the north side of the Green, the main rebel positions along the west. Jimmy now was on the east side: the only bullets that might come his way would be stray ones. Nevertheless he crouched as he ran, because a stray bullet would do just as much harm as an aimed one if it hit him. Private Martin, when he took care as he crossed Burgh Quay, Jimmy realised, was not being too cautious, only sensible: Jimmy understood that now.

He ran until he came to the Green's south-eastern corner. Then he stopped.

What am I doing? he asked himself. What am I doing?

But he knew, really, what he was doing, though he hadn't consciously decided to do it. If he turned right here he would reach the corner where he had met Mick on Monday. What he'd do when he got there he didn't know, but the rebel positions would be only a few yards away.

Jimmy thought about Mick and about his guess that Mick didn't expect to come out of this rebellion alive. He decided he had to try to find him. He started to run again, towards the College of Surgeons. A haze of dark gunsmoke hung in the air in front of the college, and through this haze Jimmy saw the flashes of the rebel guns.

It was strange and deserted at this side of the Green. A line of tram cars stood abandoned in a nearby street. Jimmy saw nobody moving. This was a dangerous place. There was real death in the air around the Green, death in the form of stray or aimed bullets flying invisibly through the air. The bullets didn't care what they hit. It wasn't their job to think.

'Conway! You! Conway!' The shout came during a lull in the firing. It came from somewhere nearby.

Jimmy looked around him, terrified. Had he imagined it?

'Blast you, boy! Conway!'

Still Jimmy couldn't see where the shouting was coming from. He looked around him again. The voice uttered a string of curses.

'Lord help us!' the voice said. 'The whole family is stupid!'

And then Jimmy saw the source of the voice. At the other end of the barricade by which he stood, and from its other side, a head was looking at him from behind a cart. It was a big head, wearing a battered bowler hat. The hair on the head, and the big moustache on the face, were fiery red, as was the face itself. The head belonged to Jimmy's uncle – though he preferred to think of him just as Ella's husband – Charlie Fox.

Beside the red face now Jimmy saw the strained white knuckles of Charlie's hands. He was holding himself up by gripping the edges of the cart, and the features of the red face were twisted as if in pain. Charlie must be wounded!

'Blast you, boy!' he gasped. 'Get over here and help me!'

It was obvious that pain had done nothing to change

Charlie's usual temper. Jimmy didn't know him well, but he didn't like him. He was an unpleasant man, who hated his wife's relatives and made no secret of it. Still, he was a relative – sort of – and he needed help. Jimmy hardly hesitated before stepping towards him.

Before he even reached Charlie Jimmy knew something was odd. He could literally smell it. What he smelled was an overpowering stink of whiskey, and it seemed to be coming from Charlie Fox.

'You took your damned time,' Charlie snarled. His voice was thick.

There was no sign on Charlie of any wound at all. It was obvious now what was wrong with him: Charlie was drunk! Completely drunk, at nine o'clock in the morning!

'Well?' he gasped. 'Are you going to help me?'

Jimmy tried to control his anger. He thought of Mick, fighting now for what he believed in, just a few yards away from this very barricade. He thought of Ma, who by now would be awake and worrying. Then, Jimmy thought of Ella. Maybe if he helped Charlie home ...

Charlie's rough hand grabbed his coat.

'Damned woman threw me out when the money was gone,' Charlie slurred. 'When I'd spent it all ...'

He was talking about some bar owner, Jimmy guessed, or someone in a shebeen, one of the city's illegal drinking places. Charlie's hat had fallen off, but he didn't seem to notice. He was on Jimmy's side of the barricade now, holding onto Jimmy, hauling himself up.

Jimmy swayed under Charlie's weight. The coins in his pocket jingled. Charlie dragged him savagely forward.

'What's that?' he demanded. Suddenly he was not so helpless. From close up, the smell of drink made Jimmy nearly sick. 'Where did you get money, you little thief?'

Jimmy tried to stammer an answer; he thought it best to say nothing about soldiers. 'M-M-Mick ...' he began.

Charlie hit him hard in the face. 'Don't lie to me, you whelp,' Charlie growled. 'Your fine rebel uncle has no money left. I've spent it – he won't need it on the gallows, where he's going. Now where did you get money? Stole it, I suppose, like he did.'

Jimmy felt tears in his eyes, and he couldn't see properly. One part of his mind, though, felt very clear and very angry. Charlie had taken Mick's money, not Ella! He'd taken Mick's money, and over the past two days he'd spent it all on drink. Four pounds! No wonder he smelled so foul.

'You spent four whole pounds?' Jimmy gasped.

'I wish I had,' groaned Charlie. 'But your stupid aunt wasted half of it on food – for your lot, if you don't mind. The whole kitchen full of food to give away, and me dying with the thirst! I taught her a lesson she won't forget, I tell you!'

Food! The word struck Jimmy like a bolt of lightning.

Charlie was standing erect now, holding Jimmy up by

the collar of his coat with one hand so that the boy's feet no longer touched the ground. As Jimmy opened swollen lips to say something more, Charlie hit him in the face again with his free hand. The man was mad with drink.

'You little rebel thief!' he said. 'Give me that money!'

Jimmy's head was spinning. Charlie had robbed Mick's money, and now he wanted Jimmy's! Jimmy drew back one foot as far as it would go. Charlie didn't notice. Then, with all of his strength, Jimmy lashed out and kicked him in the stomach.

Charlie noticed that, all right. He roared like a bull, dropped Jimmy immediately and clawed at his stomach. Coins from Jimmy's pocket scattered on the roadway, but Jimmy didn't stop to pick them up. It was time to run.

Behind him he heard Charlie roaring curses, and then his heavy steps in pursuit. Jimmy had kicked him with his full strength, but it was only the strength of a weak and undernourished boy.

Jimmy didn't get far. He was jerked from his feet as Charlie's heavy hand clamped down on his collar. Behind him Charlie's wordless roar of hate and pain sounded louder than the nearby gunfire.

There was another blow, to the back of Jimmy's head this time. Behind him Charlie gave a great screaming yell. It sounded less like anger than agony. Jimmy was flung to the ground. He hit his head on the road.

Am I shot? he wondered.

A great crushing weight landed on his back. All of his breath left his body as he screamed. All consciousness went, as if someone had switched it off.

16

RESURRECTION AND FAILURE

AN OLD WOMAN CHASED HIM down an endless corridor. She wore a black shawl. Her hair was green and there was blood at the sides of her mouth. At length she cornered him and advanced, smiling. There was more blood on her teeth and gums, as though she'd been eating raw meat.

'Give us a kiss, love,' she said.

Her smile grew wider and wider. Then her face fell off, and shattered into pieces when it hit the floor.

Jimmy woke from the awful dream. He opened his eyes and looked at a blank ceiling. Was he dead? If so, was this heaven? If not, was it ...

A woman leaned over him. Young. Her hair wasn't green. 'How do you feel?' she asked.

Jimmy blinked. He was lying on his back, on what felt like a table or a very hard bed. 'I'm alive!' he said.

The woman smiled at the surprise in his voice. 'Can you sit up?' she asked.

She helped him. The room seemed to swim in front of

his eyes. It was not a room he knew.

'Where am I?' he asked.

'This is Hume Street Hospital,' the woman said. She was, he saw now, dressed in a nurse's uniform.

'What happened to me?' he asked her.

'Someone ... fell on you,' she answered.

Jimmy looked at her sharply – she was leaving something out. 'Charlie,' he said. 'My uncle Charlie.'

He remembered now what had happened, and tried to make sense of it. 'Was he shot?' he asked the nurse. The calmness in his voice surprised him. He might have been asking her about the weather. The woman hesitated.

'He was,' said Jimmy with certainty.

She nodded.

Jimmy looked down at his body. He was sitting, dressed in his own clothes, on a bed-like trolley. He could see no sign of a wound.

'I'm not shot, though, am I?' he asked.

'No,' the nurse said. She sounded happier talking about this. 'I'm told that the man ... that your uncle ... was hitting you and shouting. He was holding you up off the ground. Then he was shot, and he dropped you. You landed on your head. Then he fell on top of you.'

'He was drunk,' Jimmy said. 'He spent my Ma's money on drink then he wanted my money too.'

'Oh!' said the nurse. 'I see.'

She seemed embarrassed, and Jimmy wondered

whether it was his own matter-of-fact tone that made her feel awkward. The tone reflected his feelings. He could find no grief in himself at the news of Charlie's death.

'I'm not hurt, then?' he asked.

'You have a high temperature. Your face is swollen too – where your uncle hit you, I suppose.'

His face did feel puffy, and his whole body ached. Worse again, his head felt hot and confused. He hoped that was an effect of the beating, but it did feel like he was getting sick, and he couldn't afford that.

How long had he been unconscious? He had no way of knowing. The blinds in the room were drawn. From nearby came the sound of gunfire. Jimmy was suddenly afraid.

'What time is it?' he asked.

'Three o'clock,' the nurse said. 'We thought it best to let you wake up naturally. It's always the safest way.'

Jimmy wasn't listening. Three o'clock? He had been unconscious for six hours! Anything could have happened!

'So if I'm not hurt,' he said, 'I can go.'

'Well, there's your temperature,' she said. 'And you did get a very nasty bang on your head when you hit the road. You might have concussion, or shock. You do seem to be all right now, only ... your coat is ruined.'

From a chair she picked up the overcoat he'd found in Old Abbey Street. The coins still left in the pocket jingled.

The coat was covered with dried mud and blood, Charlie's blood.

'Maybe you should stay here for a while,' the nurse said. 'Till we find out if that temperature goes down. When you get a knock on the head, the effects can take a while to show.'

'No,' said Jimmy firmly. 'I must go. My Ma will be worried sick about me.'

It wasn't a lie – she would certainly be worried about him. The nurse looked undecided, but they were busy here, looking after lots of wounded people. Finally she nodded.

'Yes,' she said. 'I'm sure she will be worried. What about your coat?'

Jimmy shrugged. 'I'll never wear it again,' he said, looking at the stains.

The nurse blushed, feeling that she'd been insensitive. 'No,' she said. 'But there's money in the pocket.'

'Yes. My money and my mouth organ. Could you take them out for me?'

'Of course.'

She pulled out the coins and handed them to him. Jimmy stuffed them in the pocket of his own old jacket. Only some of the money had fallen on the ground when Charlie tried to take it; most of it seemed to be still here. The nurse handed him the harmonica, and he put that in his other pocket. As Jimmy put it away, he felt something

118

in the bottom of his pocket already. It was the chocolate that the young Volunteer had given him that morning. He'd forgotten all about it.

'Have there been many civilians shot?' he asked the nurse.

'Yes,' she said. 'Too many.'

Any at all, Jimmy thought, was too many. Soldiers went out to fight – it was their job. But ordinary people just went about their business, and the bullets hit them anyway. It wasn't fair.

Although he tried to hide it from the nurse as he left, Jimmy still felt dizzy and confused. He hoped that it was just the result of Charlie's clouts, but he'd been sick often enough to know what sickness felt like, and at the back of his mind now a single word had formed itself: fever. He tried to put the thought out of his mind. If he was coming down with Sarah's fever then he was in very big trouble indeed.

Hume Street hospital was just off the eastern side of the Green. Jimmy had been listening to the gunfire since waking. He'd heard, too, the occasional distant sound of the artillery. By now the shooting seemed almost a natural part of the city's sounds. But when he got out into the open air he noticed that the sounds were different now after all.

At first, hearing the artillery, he'd thought it was the gunboat still shelling Liberty Hall. That did seem odd: six hours of shelling would have reduced the building to rubble, even if no-one had noticed that it was empty. Now he realised that there was more than one big gun firing. He could only think that they'd started bombarding the Post Office. He shivered at the thought.

He stood outside the hospital undecided, trying to make some sense from the sounds he was hearing. As he stood, he ate the chocolate he'd been given so many hours before. It had softened in his pocket, and lost its shape, but it tasted wonderful.

No mere taste could cheer Jimmy up now though. Inside he was devastated. He'd been unconscious for six solid hours. It was the middle of the afternoon, and he hadn't even got close to Ella's. And he hadn't found out about Mick either.

Of course he knew now that there was no money in Ella's, but there was food. That was even better. The whole kitchen full, Charlie had said, and all meant for the Conways. He was still more than half way to her house. It would be foolish to go back when he was so close. The fighting was getting worse: he might not get another chance.

A man was walking up Hume Street towards him. Jimmy ran over to him. 'Mister!' he said. 'Mister! I have to go to Northumberland Road. Do you know if there's fighting there?'

'Don't even think about it,' the man said. 'Northumberland Road is like a slaughterhouse. I saw it from Mount

Street. The British came marching up it, and the fellows laid into them. There's no way you'll get the

Those six lost hours had ruined everything, Jimmy realised. The fighting had started in exactly the place that he wanted to go: he'd missed his chance. He shivered, and a hot flush spread over his body. He felt sick.

'Go home, lad,' advised the man. 'Get in off the streets.'

'If I can get home,' Jimmy said bitterly.

'You'll have to get in somewhere before nightfall anyway,' the man said. 'The British have declared a curfew: everyone is to be off the streets before dark. Otherwise they'll be shot at.'

At the back of his mind Jimmy had been wondering whether he might somehow hang around till the fighting in Northumberland Road died down. Now even that seemed impossible.

'I must be away,' the man said. 'Off home with you now, sonny, if you've any sense.'

Jimmy nodded dumbly. He felt too bad to speak. Maybe there really was nothing else he could do now except get home safely. He *had* managed to get a little money, but it would be useless with no shops open.

He thought of the journey back across the river. That too would be dangerous. Then he thought of all that food at Ella's. He was so close now. Why not risk going on? He had little to lose and everything to gain.

TRAPPED

TO GET TO ELLA'S, JIMMY would have to cross the Grand Canal. He set off immediately, before he had time to be frightened. His head hurt and his body felt heavy and strange, but he kept thinking of that kitchen full of food.

He walked quickly down Mount Street. At its far end lay the Grand Canal, and on the other side of the bridge was – finally – Northumberland Road.

There was heavy firing going on down towards the canal and it grew louder as he approached. There was no boom of artillery, but what sounded like hundreds of rifles keeping up a continuous fire. It was an endless, rolling wave, like a distant storm.

A large crowd of civilians had gathered at the top of Mount Street; they blocked his view of the bridge beyond. It was strange, but in a way it was cheering – things couldn't be so bad if all these people were standing around, could they? The shooting seemed to be coming from directly ahead, beyond the crowd.

One of the things that surprised Jimmy most during the day was the constant presence of onlookers. The people of Dublin were reacting to the rebellion in odd ways. In places they were calm, and went about their business as best they could. But wherever there was fighting going on people gathered around to watch. They treated it like entertainment, as if they couldn't really believe that it was serious. Certainly they didn't seem to believe that they themselves might be in danger.

The onlookers gave the whole rebellion a strange air of fantasy. If this was a serious fight, it seemed, these people wouldn't be standing around so casually watching it. Again and again Jimmy found himself thinking of the crowd as spectators at a sports match. You nearly expected them to start clapping after some especially clever shot or move made by one side or the other. It was all like some strange and sinister dream.

This crowd was the biggest he'd seen watching any of the fighting. At its rear, even more strangely, a tramp with a big bushy beard was playing a fiddle, hoping to collect some coppers. But the people ignored him, too busy watching the scene that Jimmy still couldn't see. As Jimmy drew near there was a lull in the gunfire. A stir came from the crowd, but Jimmy couldn't make out what was happening. Then the crowd parted in several places and people appeared carrying large bundles. It took several people to carry each bundle.

Jimmy stopped, mystified. Then he noticed that the bundles were a khaki colour, that they were in fact dead or wounded soldiers. The people carried the soldiers down a laneway, towards a first-aid station.

He was beside the fiddle player now. The tramp stopped playing his fiddle and gestured at the hurrying people.

'A terrible fight,' he said. 'A terrible fight to be sure.'

A whistle blew somewhere ahead, and the shooting started again. It sounded for all the world like a referee's whistle. Was he going mad? But there was nothing imaginary about the renewed storm of fire that answered the whistle.

'What's happening?' he asked the tramp.

The man shrugged and spat on the ground. 'Somebody is shooting somebody else,' he said, 'and the public is enjoying the free entertainment – so they're neglecting me.' He smiled at Jimmy. 'I don't suppose, young fellow,' he said, 'that you'd have a spare copper? You don't look as if you do, but there's no harm in asking.'

Jimmy was looking beyond him, at the back of the crowd. He reached absentmindedly into his pocket and pulled out a coin. He handed it to the tramp, who looked at it in surprise.

'Sixpence!' he said. 'Glory be! The poor give to the poor – it's the way of the world.'

But Jimmy wasn't really paying any attention to him. He hadn't even noticed that he was giving the man so much money. Instead he ran past the tramp, worming his way through the motionless crowd towards the bridge.

His head hurt now, and his throat felt sore. He was definitely sick. He stepped on several feet as he passed through the crowd, but nobody paid any attention to him. They were all transfixed by the scene in front of them.

Nothing he'd come across since Monday had prepared Jimmy for what he saw when he finally reached the front of the crowd. It was a sight so terrible that it held him as mesmerised as any of the other watchers. He had only imagined that he'd seen terrible things since Monday: compared to this, everything else had been only a small horror. What was happening on Mount Street Bridge was the worst thing in the world.

18

MOUNT STREET BRIDGE

WHEN HE SAW THE SOLDIERS ON THE BRIDGE Jimmy thought that they must be troops from the barracks at Beggar's Bush. The barracks was just down the road. It seemed natural that they'd march this way if they were going into the city.

In fact the soldiers were not from the barracks. They'd come over from Britain the night before. From the harbour at Kingstown three columns of troops had marched the six miles into Dublin. Two of the columns had taken other routes, and they'd already entered the city with no resistance. The third column came as far as Mount Street Bridge and didn't look as though they were going to get any farther.

The Irish Volunteers had taken over two houses in Northumberland Road itself, and a third, Clanwilliam House, on the city side of the canal overlooking Mount Street Bridge. They'd ambushed the third column as it came, and the fighting had been going on all morning.

Later Jimmy learned that there were only about a dozen Volunteers involved; but looking at the shooting, you'd think there were hundreds of Volunteers there. They had no heavy arms, only rifles and pistols. They didn't have a single bomb or grenade between them. But they were in a perfect ambush position, and the British army had brought its men over in such a hurry that they had no bombs or grenades either. They were regretting that now. And they were dying because of it.

All the soldiers could do was to attack the Volunteer positions, and all the Volunteers had to do was to keep firing. They hardly even needed to aim. The result was like something from a slaughterhouse. The soldiers charged the bridge, the Volunteers shot them down as they charged.

Jimmy heard the facts of the matter later, when the rebellion was over; he even met one of the men who'd been in Clanwilliam House. Now, at four o'clock on that day, he had no thought of facts or statistics. He'd been thinking a lot about dying during the day; now he was watching death having a party. It seemed as though hundreds of young men were being slaughtered in front of his eyes. It was madness.

To his left Jimmy heard the thunder of the Volunteers' guns from Clanwilliam House, but his eyes stayed fixed in front of him on Mount Street Bridge. The bridge, and Northumberland Road beyond, seemed to be a solid mass of soldiers. Some of them were upright, running; others were crawling, and many were just lying still, unable to move.

The whistle that Jimmy had heard was the signal for a charge. Soldiers on the footpaths of Northumberland Road, still unsure of just how many houses the Volunteers held, were pouring fire into every house where anything moved. Past them charged a great khaki wave of men heading for the bridge. They were trying to cross it, to reach the Volunteers' position on the other side of the canal.

But they were failing completely. It was as if someone had drawn an invisible line about halfway across the bridge, a line that meant death for anyone who tried to cross it.

The troops charged up the road. When they reached the bridge they threw themselves on the ground and began to crawl. The roadway and footpaths of the bridge itself were completely covered with crawling men. They wormed along in column, forming what looked to Jimmy's feverish eyes like four giant, khaki-coloured snakes. Between these snakes, and all around them, lay the dead and wounded. The snakes, as they tried to advance, added their share to these piles.

No-one got beyond that midway point. Again and again Jimmy saw crawling soldiers drop and lie still, or jump up screaming, only to flop brokenly back down. It was, indeed, a slaughter. And this was all happening only a few yards in front of the watching crowd. Here were the civilians, watching, while a few yards away were these hundreds of men crawling, crying, screaming and dying.

'The poor boys,' said a stout woman in a white apron beside Jimmy. 'The poor young fellas.'

Jimmy's whole body trembled as he stood. He wanted to run away, to scream himself; but his feet wouldn't move and his voice stuck in his throat. He was as frozen as any of the dead young men on the bridge. He couldn't even make his eyes close, though he dearly wanted to close them.

Ahead of him the bridge bristled with khaki figures. They jerked and tossed like the leaves of a tree being blown in a strong wind. But they weren't leaves, they were men: they were fathers and brothers and sons and uncles. They were good men or bad men, mean or decent men, heroes or cowards.

The wind that tossed them didn't care what they were. It was the same wind that had hit Charlie Fox, that had sent Billy Moran tumbling to the grass in the Green. It was the wind of death, and it was snuffing these men's lives out like so many candles.

Finally they stopped coming. The shooting in Northumberland Road went on, but the Volunteers in Clanwilliam House stopped firing. To Jimmy's astonishment, people from the crowd around him began to run out on to the bridge. There was a priest, and a man in a white coat who must be a doctor. There was a small group of other men and women too. The civilians on the bridge bent to the wounded soldiers. They helped those who could still walk to get to their feet. The other wounded had to be carried.

'Clear the way,' people shouted. 'Clear the way there!'

Three men carrying a soldier with a headwound staggered past Jimmy. The crowd made way for them. More wounded, alone or else supported or carried by onlookers, streamed by. It was another procession such as Jimmy had seen as he arrived. He watched them disappearing into the laneway behind Clanwilliam House.

From Northumberland Road the whistle blew again. The last civilians were sprinting hastily from the bridge. Up along Northumberland Road, another wave of soldiers was rushed towards the canal.

Oh no, Jimmy thought. Please, no. Not again.

With tears in his eyes, unable to make himself move, he was forced to watch the same awful scene repeat itself. The first soldiers fell without even reaching the bridge. Those who did reach it threw themselves down and began to crawl forward, forming once more into the huge, ugly snakes. The Volunteers picked them off like flies. Not one soldier got more than halfway across. The piles of bodies grew higher. It was like watching the previous attack all over again.

'Mother of mercy,' said the stout woman beside him. 'Those poor, poor boys.'

Had this, then, been going on since morning? It made no difference to him that the soldiers would have shot the Volunteers in the same way if the positions had been reversed. The point was that nobody should do this to anybody at all.

Beside him Jimmy heard a sudden gasp and a muffled cry. The stout woman in the apron crumpled and fell to the ground. At first Jimmy thought she'd fainted, but then he saw the spreading red stain on the white apron. Someone called for a doctor. The woman lay on the ground. She looked puzzled. She opened her mouth as if to say something, but nothing came out.

'The poor young boys,' she said at last.

Something inside Jimmy snapped. Too weak to run, he staggered away and up along the canal. After a minute he had to stop. He bent over and was violently sick. His body shook. His face was burning.

If someone had asked Jimmy his name right then, he couldn't have told them. He felt he was going mad. But it wasn't madness. Nor was it the effect of Charlie's punches, although they hadn't helped. It wasn't even the growing shock he'd been feeling all day, a shock that had reached its high point watching the insanity on the bridge.

What was wrong with Jimmy now was simpler but much more dangerous than any of those things. It was what he'd feared but hadn't wanted to believe or even really think about: he'd picked up Sarah's fever, and now it had come to claim him. His body shook, and the fever burned in his brain.

Behind him, in Northumberland Road, a whistle blew; but Jimmy Conway was no longer interested in the game.

19

THE MUSICAL TRAMP

JIMMY WOULD NEVER KNOW FOR SURE just how he spent the next hour or so. His senses were too mixed up by the fever's burning. When his mind cleared briefly he found himself in Pembroke Road. Long flights of steps led up to the front doors of the houses here. Jimmy found himself sitting at the bottom of one such flight, leaning against the railings. His whole body was burning and his clothes were soaked with sweat.

In the distance he heard firing, and now explosions too. Also, the strains of fiddle music seemed to float down on the still air. A fiddle? Jimmy remembered something about a fiddle, but he couldn't fix the memory in his mind. Then the music stopped suddenly, and it didn't start again.

Pembroke Road itself seemed to be deserted, at least around here. Jimmy clung desperately to the railings of the house. He had to think, he told himself.

Footsteps came down the road. A man was coming from the direction of the bridge. He wore a ragged overcoat and had long, unkempt hair and a big bushy beard. Jimmy was certain he'd seen him before but he couldn't think where.

As the man came closer Jimmy heard him muttering to himself. Behind the thick beard his face looked miserable. He reached Jimmy and, seeing the boy's blank stare, stopped beside him and stared back.

'Well hello,' the man said finally. 'It's the generous poor young man, ain't it?'

A memory struggled into Jimmy's mind – this man had been playing music somewhere.

'I ...' he began. It was hard to talk. His throat burned. His tongue felt too big for his mouth. He forced the words out. 'I'm sick.'

The tramp looked at him with some sympathy. 'You

don't look well, right enough,' he said. 'The whole city is sick if you ask me.'

He reached into the deep pockets of his ragged coat and pulled out two handfuls of little sticks. Mixed in with the sticks were what looked like pieces of wire.

'Do you know what this is?' the man demanded.

Jimmy tried to focus his eyes. Some of the sticks were hardly bigger than matches. 'Is it kindling?' he asked.

The tramp snorted with scorn. Then, considering, he sighed. 'Aye,' he said. 'I suppose it is – now. But do you know what it was?'

Jimmy shook his head. The tramp seemed to waver in front of his eyes.

'That was my fiddle,' the tramp said sadly. 'A fine fiddle that I got in county Kerry nearly twenty years ago now. I'm after using it to earn me bread since, all over this country. And today I was using it for the same thing – if there is any bread left in this cursed city.' The tramp spat on the ground. 'Divil a ha'penny I got today, barring yer tanner.' The tramp seemed angry now. 'I played them patriotic British marching songs and good Irish rebel songs, but they were all far too busy watching men slaughtering each other to listen. Good loyal citizens all – bad cess to them! – and to the soldiers too.

'So then this big ugly British sergeant,' the tramp went on, unstoppable now he had an audience, 'told me to move on. I'll remember that cur for as long as I live. I let me temper get the better of me,' he said. 'You'd think I'd know better at my age. I asked the big bosthoon who he thought he was, an English lout, to be telling an Irishman to move on in his own country. And with that he snatched me poor darlin' little fiddle and trampled it under his big clodhopping army boots. Trampled it into ... into kindling, as you so cleverly put it.'

Sighing again, he looked at the pathetic bundles of splinters in his hands. Then he put each bundle carefully back in his pockets.

'All me own fault, of course,' he said. 'I can't hould me tongue sometimes – I'm the first to admit it. But the gall of the man!'

Jimmy forced himself to ask a question. 'Why,' he asked slowly, 'are you keeping the pieces?'

The tramp thought for a moment. 'Why, to start a fire with,' he said. 'Waste not, want not! You know, boy, with me fiddle, I was an entertainer; without it I'm only a beggar here, and that's no thing to be in this town. The wars of ould Empire's glory are after leaving too many crippled soldiers in Dublin. What chance do I have against that kind of competition? The European war will ruin the trade entirely – and this local skirmish won't help either.'

Jimmy didn't follow all that the tramp said, but he warmed to the man.

'W ... where do you live?' he asked him.

'I have a little tent – a sort of a tent, I should say. But it's dry at least, or at least it's sort of dry. A humble thing, but my own. It's down there be the river Dodder, if the army aren't after bombing it as a rebel stronghold. They seem to be shooting at anything they don't understand, and soldiers don't understand much. I should get back there now, too. It'll be dark soon, and there's a curfew. Losing me fiddle to the army is bad enough, but losing me life to them would be worse.'

Jimmy tried to think clearly. He remembered suddenly why he himself must get off the streets. Would the tramp shelter him if he offered him some of the money that he still had? He ought to keep it for his family, but it would be no use to them anyway if the army shot him in the dark.

But if the tramp found out he had the money there was nothing to stop him from just taking it and leaving Jimmy where he was. Nobody would care. Nobody would believe that a poor boy like Jimmy had money anyway, unless he'd robbed it himself.

The boy struggled to decide what he should do, but he just couldn't think. The fever and the dizziness came in waves and washed his thoughts away, like the waves washing things off a beach. The effort to hold on to them was painful. Jimmy groaned.

Hearing the groan, the tramp leaned forward and peered into the boy's face. 'You really are sick, young fella,' he announced. He reached out and touched

Jimmy's forehead. 'Fever,' he said. 'You're burning up with it! What are you doing out at all, at all?'

Jimmy tried to explain, but the effort was too much. The tramp heard the words 'no food' and 'Ma'. They were enough to tell him that the boy was in real trouble, but then you didn't need much imagination to see that.

'Can you play the mouth organ?' asked Jimmy suddenly. The words came out in a rush.

The tramp frowned, puzzled. The boy was raving; the fever had addled his brain. What should he do with him? It was probably some child's condition that would be harmless to the tramp himself – in his time he had had every fever going. The chances were that this one would be powerless against him. In any case the child couldn't be left here: he'd get no help from anyone living in this area.

'The mouth organ,' Jimmy asked again, with an effort. 'Can you play it?'

The tramp decided to humour him. 'Of course I can,' he said. 'A man that can play a fiddle can play a thing as simple as a mouth organ. The French fiddle, some calls it – though that's an awful insult to fiddles, and an awful insult to French people too, for all I know.'

'Shelter me till the morning,' Jimmy said, 'and I'll give you a brand new mouth organ. Then you won't be a beggar.'

The tramp could hear the desperation in the boy's

voice, and his heart went out to the child. He was obviously raving about the mouth organ. But there's a kind of brotherhood in misery – to abandon him here would be a crime.

'Come on,' he said to Jimmy. 'You have to get in someplace anyhow.'

The boy pushed himself up from the steps and tried to stand up. He swayed from side to side. 'Is it far?' he managed to ask.

The tramp looked at him with pity. 'Here, lean on me,' he offered. 'You won't get far on your own.'

Jimmy did as he was told, glad of the adult support. With the tramp's arm around him he felt safer. After a day of terrible danger he'd had to face alone, he was sick, lonely, hungry, tired and worried.

Stumbling slowly down Pembroke Road Jimmy felt better. Even though the fever visions racked him, he felt that there might, after all, be some goodness left in the world.

20

THE LOST DAY

THE NEXT THING JIMMY REMEMBERED was waking briefly some time in the middle of the night, though what night it was he didn't know. He was lying under a pile of ragged blankets and the tramp was leaning over him, calling softly to him.

Jimmy tried to answer, but his mouth was too dry to speak. The tramp gave him some water, and told him that his fever had broken during the night.

The man wiped the boy's forehead with a cloth soaked in river water, and after that Jimmy passed out again. Later – it was light this time – he was woken again by the tramp shaking him gently.

'I'm going out,' the tramp said. 'There's a woman up the road who gives me food sometimes. I'm going to ask her for something now. There's nothing left here.'

Jimmy nodded weakly. He closed his eyes. When he opened them again the tramp was gone, but Jimmy had no way of knowing whether he had slept again or simply blinked. He sat up. He felt weak and helpless, but the fever seemed to be gone.

Jimmy looked around at the tramp's home. It was a rough structure made of canvas that was supported by a framework of sticks. Outside Jimmy could hear birds singing, and the sound of running water that must be the river Dodder. In the distance too there was some shooting.

It was dark and shadowy inside the makeshift tent. Through a crack in the canvas Jimmy saw that it was sunny outside. He wondered how long he'd been asleep – it might be Thursday now for all that he knew. His mother would be half crazy with worry.

His tiredness made him want to lie down again. It would be grand just to sleep – to sleep for days and days and wake up rested and recovered. But already worry was nagging at him. Fever or no fever, it amounted to the same thing: he had wasted more time.

He made himself get up from under the blankets. He found the low entrance to the tent and crawled outside.

He was on a grassy site by a bridge over the river. The tent had been set up in the shelter of some low trees. Looking at it from outside, Jimmy thought how ramshackle it looked. It must have been terrible to live here in winter – worse than any slum room.

Jimmy waited for a while, hoping the tramp would come back. He wanted to thank him. But there was no sign of the musical tramp, and Jimmy could feel himself growing weaker even as he stood waiting. He would have to leave soon. He had to find out what was going on.

He went briefly back inside the little tent. It seemed dank and bad-smelling now, after the sunlight and fresh air outside. Apart from the pile of ragged blankets it was empty. The tramp seemed to have no possessions at all. Jimmy thought for a moment, then searched in his pockets. The money and the mouth organ were still there. He counted the remaining coins: four shillings and twopence. Counting the sixpence that he'd given yesterday to the tramp, that meant he'd only lost a few pennies in his struggle with Charlie.

Jimmy counted out two shillings in pennies and threepenny bits. He put the two shillings, with the mouth organ, under the pile of blankets. The tramp would find it later on, if nobody came and stole it first. Jimmy doubted that anyone would: nobody would think there was anything worth stealing in such a place.

When he crawled back outside he felt weaker than ever. But he was able to think clearly again, and that seemed more important than physical strength. Jimmy had no idea of exactly where he was, and saw nobody that he might ask. The road beside him must lead back to somewhere in Ballsbridge. He would have to chance it. He started up the road in what seemed the most likely direction.

He saw the two soldiers just as he crossed a railway line. They were standing by the side of the road. They had fixed bayonets on their rifles, but they didn't seem to be very cautious. They watched him approach without any sign of interest.

'Hello,' said Jimmy, making himself smile. Just stay out of trouble, he told himself.

'Hello yourself,' one soldier said in an English accent.

'How is the fighting going?' Jimmy asked.

The second soldier laughed. 'Listen to that,' he said. 'Bloodthirsty little fellow, isn't he?'

'No,' said Jimmy. 'Just afraid.' That was true enough, he thought.

'Well, the fighting's not over yet,' the first soldier said. 'But it soon will be. We're in control of the city. We'll soon have them out.'

'They'd be out already,' grumbled the other soldier, 'if the officers weren't so damned cautious. It's a disgrace to let this thing go into a fifth day.'

Jimmy thought he must have heard him wrongly. A fifth day? 'Did you say a fifth day?' he asked

'Sure,' said the soldier. 'Started Monday, didn't it? This is Friday – so: five days.'

Jimmy was shocked. 'Please,' he said. 'Did you say this was *Friday*?'

The soldiers looked at each other and laughed.

'Hear that, Bob?' asked the first one. 'I told you the natives were stupid! This kid don't even know what day of the week it is!'

Jimmy ignored the mockery. He had more important

things on his mind. Could it really be Friday?

The second soldier noticed how miserable Jimmy looked, and took pity on him.

'This is Friday, son,' he said. 'Friday the twenty-eighth of April.'

Jimmy almost fainted. It was true, then. Things were even worse than he had supposed: he had lost a whole day!

Without another thought he began to run. His mother would be more than just worried: by now she must be sure that she would never see her son again.

He saw a street sign as he ran: 'Lansdowne Road', it said. That was very near Northumberland Road. He heard no shooting from there either. Something that might be hope began to grow in his heart. Perhaps, after all, he could rescue a little bit from this week of disaster.

21

NORTHUMBERLAND ROAD

HALF WAY UP NORTHUMBERLAND ROAD signs of the battle started to show. One house was completely devastated. Its windows were gone and its door blown in by explosives. The walls were stippled by bulletmarks. It must have been one of the rebel strongholds. Now it was a ruin.

Most of the other houses had smashed windows and bullet-holed doors. It seemed impossible that they'd all housed rebels. An air of fear and terror seemed to hang over the road, a silence in which no birds sang. Jimmy could feel it as he walked along.

Ella's house was several doors up from the bombed-in ruin. Jimmy walked through the open gate, hardly believing that he was finally here. This house too had taken its share of ill-treatment during the fighting. There didn't seem to be a window left unbroken in the upper storeys. When Jimmy climbed the steps and reached the front door he found it was ajar. He knocked loudly, but there was no reply. Eventually he slipped into the dim hall.

'Hello?' he called. 'Ella?'

Only echoes answered him. He hesitated. The house

seemed abandoned. Jimmy stopped in the hall for a few moments. Should he leave? Then his foolishness struck him. He'd left home three days ago to come to this house. Since then he'd been through terror, fever and danger. It would be stupid not to search for the food now that he was finally here.

There were three families living in the house, Jimmy knew. Three couples, rather – where Jimmy came from, that wasn't regarded as a family. Families had children.

Ella and Charlie lived on the ground floor, where Jimmy was standing. On the top floor and in the basement lived two older couples. There was a stairs facing Jimmy in the hall where he stood, and at the top of the stairs was a closed door. One of the old couples must live behind it. To either side of him was another door, and the rooms behind these would belong to Charlie and Ella. So they had more than one room: Jimmy had suspected as much.

He tried the door on his right. It opened into a parlour full of furniture. There was a big window with a table standing in front of it. The table and the floor around it were covered with broken glass from the bullet-shattered window. Bullets had knocked lumps of plaster from the wall and broken the glass on a picture of the king that hung there. A layer of dust from the smashed plaster lay over all of the furniture.

Jimmy looked fearfully around the floor, half expecting to see a body lying there; but the floor was bare except for bits of glass and plaster.

He closed the door and tried the one across the hall. This led into a dining room and kitchen. Here too the window was broken, the walls pitted and pockmarked with bullets. But it wasn't the damage that caught Jimmy's eye; it was the big cupboard standing open by the far wall.

The cupboard was obviously Ella's larder. There were five shelves inside it, and all five of the shelves were simply stuffed with food. There were cans and packets and boxes and jars; there were parcels wrapped in brown paper. There was even a whole ham lying on a plate under a glass cover.

Jimmy's stomach rumbled as he stood looking into the cupboard. He was spellbound. He'd never seen so much food in one place outside of a shop. He had to stop himself from falling on the food there and then. The last thing he recalled eating was the piece of chocolate on Wednesday afternoon. If the tramp had succeeded in feeding him anything since, Jimmy had forgotten it.

His mouth watered, but he controlled himself. First he must find out what was going on. He must, if he could, find Ella. He must at least find out where she was. Then he'd help himself to the food. In this new excitement, he'd almost forgotten his tiredness.

At the back of this room there was another door which led to a bedroom. This too was deserted. There were clothes in the wardrobe: if Ella had left then she hadn't taken much with her.

Jimmy went back out to the hall. He climbed the stairs and knocked on the door there, but nobody answered. Next Jimmy went out the front door and down the steps to the basement. He knocked on the door there too. This time he was in luck: after the knock, he heard footsteps approaching from inside. The door opened, and an old woman looked out smiling.

'Yes, dear?' she said.

'My name is Jimmy Conway,' Jimmy said. 'I'm ...'

But the old woman interrupted him. 'You're Ella's sister's boy,' she said. Her smile widened. Jimmy was surprised.

'I ... yes, I am,' he said.

The old woman opened the door wide. 'Come in, child,' she said. 'Come in, and welcome. Would you like a cup of tea? I've just made some. My name is Mrs Breen.'

Jimmy didn't really want to go in, but the mention of tea drew him like a magnet: where there was tea there might be more food. The old woman shut the door behind him. She led him into her kitchen and sat him at the table. Then she poured him a cup of tea and gave him a huge slice of cake on a plate. Jimmy's mouth watered as he looked at the cake. He ate it as politely as he could, while the old woman smiled at him. When he had finished the cake she gave him a second slice that was even bigger.

'It's wonderful to see a boy with a good appetite,' she said. 'My husband and I don't eat much. I've had no-one to cook for since my own boys left home, and that's long ago now.'

This part of the building had, it seemed, escaped damage. It was below the level of the garden, and had been protected from the bullets. Jimmy ate the second piece of cake as he looked around. It went as quickly as the first. It was a rich cake, with currants and raisins in it. The old woman's face glowed with pleasure as she watched him eat.

'Did Ella send you to tell me that she'd got to your house safely?' she asked him.

Jimmy could only stare at her. Ella had gone to his home? He could hardly believe it. Something about the old woman's voice when she mentioned Ella made Jimmy think that she liked his aunt. The idea that anyone might like Ella hadn't entered his head in years. Ma and Mick made excuses for her, of course, but that was different: she was their sister.

The old woman didn't notice his confusion. 'It was very nice of Ella if she did send you down,' she said. 'And very nice of you to take the trouble, I'm sure. I was worried about her, as I'm sure she knew I would be – Ella is so thoughtful.'

Again Jimmy was shocked. Ella thoughtful? Maybe the woman and he weren't thinking of the same person at all?

Maybe he'd got the wrong address, and someone else called Ella lived here.

'How did you know she was my aunt?' he asked.

'Why,' said the woman, 'she's always talking about the three fine children that her sister Lily has. She always wanted to bring you on a visit, or to spend more time with you, but that husband of hers is an animal. He'll hardly let her out of the house, except when he's too drunk to notice.'

So they were talking about the same person after all. 'Charlie is dead,' Jimmy said. 'He was shot.'

The old woman looked hard at him. She sighed. 'God forgive me,' she said, 'but I can't feel very sorry. I know I should, but he was a terrible man. He was a devil. Your poor aunt had no real life with him at all.'

In a way it cheered Jimmy to meet such an honest woman. If this old lady thought Ella had sent him back with a message, he thought, it might be wise to let her go on thinking that; then, looking at her open, smiling face, he found it hard to lie to her.

In the end he found himself telling her the truth about his adventures. After she'd told him how brave he was, Mrs Breen had her own story to tell, a story that was as big a surprise to Jimmy as any he'd had all week. It was a story whose main character was Ella, but it was an Ella Jimmy hardly recognised.

It turned out that Mrs Breen knew all about Mick's

missing money. 'Ella meant to take it to your mother first thing,' she explained. 'But then it struck her that the shops would be shut if there was fighting. The money would be useless. So she spent two pounds on food. She knew that food would be more useful.

'But then Charlie came home. Ella hadn't said anything to him about the money, because she knew he'd take it. He spent most of their money on drink. Poor Ella was always left penniless, and then he'd come in expecting food on the table. She used to borrow from your mother – that woman is a saint, from what Ella says.'

Ella had managed to hide from Charlie the fact that she had four pounds, but now she couldn't conceal all the food she'd bought.

'When Charlie saw the food,' Mrs Breen went on, 'he made her tell him everything. When he heard about the money he cursed her for wasting half of it and demanded that she give the rest to him.

'Ella refused. She said the money wasn't hers. She lived in terror of that brute, but this time she resisted. It did her no good. Charlie gave her a terrible beating and took the money anyway. Then he left.

'Myself and my husband heard the sounds of fighting from upstairs. When Charlie left we went up and found Ella unconscious on the floor. We brought her downstairs and she stayed here on Monday night. Tuesday morning early she went back upstairs, expecting to find Charlie there in a stupor like she often did. She meant to take whatever was left of the money then and go straight to your house. But Charlie wasn't there.'

Ella hadn't known what to do. By then all sorts of rumours were going around about the fighting in the city. Ella hesitated for a whole day, waiting for Charlie. Then on Wednesday she was trapped, and spent hours lying on her floor while the whole house was showered with bullets.

Mrs Carr, who lived on the top floor, was shot in the fighting. She'd gone to her window to look out when the shooting started, and the troops mistook her for a rebel sniper. Her husband cared for her as best he could till the firing ended at about ten on Wednesday night. Then ambulances came to ferry the wounded to the hospital.

'Ella was helping to put Mrs Carr into an ambulance,' Mrs Breen said, 'when the driver told her that he'd be taking Mrs Carr to Hume Street or even some hospital nearer to the city centre.

'Ella decided to take the chance. She went with the ambulance, meaning to stay in the hospital until the curfew was over next morning and then make her way to your mother's if she could. There was no way that she could take anything with her, because the ambulance was so full there was hardly room for her. But she told me that if all went well she'd come back or else send someone for the food.

'And when I heard who you were,' the old woman

concluded, 'then I was sure she'd sent you.'

So now Jimmy had food! All he had to do was get it home. 'Do you know how things are in the city?' he asked.

Mrs Breen shook her head. 'Not really,' she said. 'I know things are terrible, but that's all. There are so many rumours it's hard to know what to believe. I know the army shelled Sackville Street, and half of it must be burning by now. A lot of people were shot who had neither hand, act nor part in the Rising. Even animals – they say there's not a cat or a dog left alive in Camden Street.'

Jimmy tried to imagine Sackville Street burning, but even after these past five days he couldn't picture it. It was hard to think of a city's biggest street being simply destroyed.

'The fires light up the sky at night,' Mrs Breen said. 'You can see it from here. I'm seventy-four years of age, and I never imagined I'd see anything so terrible. I cried to think of all the poor people who might be trapped in there.'

Including his family, Jimmy thought. He put that idea out of his head straight away: there was no point in worrying about that. Not yet, anyway.

They heard the front door open, and an old man came in who was obviously Mrs Breen's husband. When Jimmy had told his story the three of them went up to Ella's, Mr Breen bringing with him two big canvas sacks. They filled both sacks from the food cupboard.

The old man tied the sacks together using a thick

leather belt that he took from the bedroom. He held the big belt out and showed it to Jimmy.

'Do you see this?' he asked. 'When Charlie was drunk he used to hit your aunt with that – with the buckle of it. She often came downstairs to us bleeding from it.'

Jimmy looked at the big metal buckle. He'd seen dockers fighting with belts like this. They'd wrap the ends of the belts around their hands and swing the heavy buckles at each other. The fights were terrible to see. It was even more terrible to think of a big man like Charlie swinging that terrible weapon at a small woman like Ella. If that was what her life at home was like then it was no wonder she'd cried so much. Almost reluctantly, Jimmy began to feel some sympathy for his aunt. It would take him a while to get used to the idea.

Mr Breen tied the ends of the belt around the necks of the filled sacks, turning the belt into a halter. He put it around Jimmy's neck so that the two sacks hung down in front of him.

'Can you carry that weight?' he asked.

Jimmy felt the great weight of the food. He was still weak, and the weight made his legs tremble. But he knew he could manage – he'd have to. After the last few days of sickness and fear he'd manage to carry them somehow, even if they weighed ten times as much.

Mrs Breen wrote a note in her neat, ladylike handwriting for Jimmy to take with him. It said that this

152

boy was carrying food from her to her sister on the north side of the river. If Jimmy was stopped by soldiers, the note would help prove he hadn't been looting.

'I'll go as far as the bridge with you,' Mr Breen said. 'Just to make sure you get past the soldiers there.'

At Mount Street Bridge, Mr Breen spoke briefly to the sergeant in charge. The sergeant seemed friendly enough and Mr Breen asked him for advice on the best route into the city. The sergeant wasn't sure of how things stood, but he told them what he knew.

'I don't think you'll have any trouble before the river anyway, sir,' he said. 'We have them on the run now. But I'm not sure if it's all over in Sackville Street yet. You'll have to ask again once you're in the city centre.'

Mr Breen made Jimmy promise that he'd be careful and that he'd visit them when all this was over, a promise Jimmy gladly gave. Watching the old man go, Jimmy felt a twinge of regret. Now he was on his own again.

His whole body still felt weak and frail, as if a sudden gust of wind would blow him away. The sacks of food were very heavy. Still, he was elated. He was going home, and he was loaded with food.

He tried to keep his mind empty of everything except the act of walking. He must ignore everything else – the soldiers and the rebels and the great, empty tiredness of his body. This was the last lap in his own personal race; he must not fall now when the finishing line was so close.

22

AT TRINITY COLLEGE

HALF AN HOUR LATER JIMMY STOOD on Nassau Street. So far no-one had challenged him. He went up Nassau Street along by the railings of Trinity College, afraid that at any moment he might be stopped and sent back. For all the soldiers knew, the sacks around his neck might hold guns or grenades: they might even shoot him first and ask questions later. But at this stage he'd rather be shot than sent back.

Still, he was neither stopped nor questioned. The soldiers paid no attention to him at all.

The sound of big guns had grown louder as he came towards the river. He knew he'd have to pass them. The gunfire seemed to come from all around him here. It was as if he stood at the eye of a storm, with thunder all around.

The heaviest firing was coming from right ahead near O'Connell Bridge. Jimmy heard the rifles and the machine-guns, and the 'crump' of the artillery. Most of the rifle fire came from the army: the heavy booming sound of a rebel rifle came only occasionally. Jimmy had heard enough shooting now to recognise the difference between the two.

The sky to the north was full of dark smoke. It hung in the air like a shroud over what could only be Sackville Street.

There was no point in waiting. Only a long sleep would ease the tiredness he felt, and if he stayed here too long it would just get harder to start off again. Even his determination couldn't keep him going forever: sleep or fear would get the better of him.

His body shook with tiredness, and the street seemed to shimmer in front of his eyes. He left the doorway, crossed the road, and set off again around the corner at Trinity College. One foot first, then the other; then the first foot again, with each step feeling as though his feet were made of lead.

Overhead, from the roof of the college, the firing was heavy and constant. Jimmy staggered on, wishing he was invisible. Looking up Westmoreland Street he saw the bridge at last.

Beyond it, Sackville Street was hidden by a blanket of smoke. Above the smoke he made out a corner of the Post Office roof. The two flags still flew there, and when he saw them still flying Jimmy felt a strange thrill of pride.

The soaring finger of Nelson's Pillar rose over the dark cloud too. Below, the smoke eddied like fog. For a moment the statue of Daniel O'Connell at the near end of Sackville Street was revealed, glaring down towards the guns as though demanding to know who was daring to attack the city. Then the smoke covered the statue again.

Around Jimmy groups of soldiers came and went, ignoring him. The sound of the guns didn't seem to disturb them: indeed, they kept looking over almost fondly at the roaring weapons. The sound of your own big guns must be comforting, Jimmy supposed, especially when you knew that your enemy didn't have any.

The buildings around echoed and magnified the roar each time one of the guns fired. Still nobody seemed to notice Jimmy. He felt like a mouse creeping through a field of giants, hoping they wouldn't look down. Each yard of progress seemed precious, but each yard also seemed to demand more steps than the last.

'Boy!' He heard the call clearly over the storm of gunfire, but he tried to pretend, even to himself, that he hadn't. There could only be one boy here. Surely they couldn't stop him now – not after all this.

He might have tried to run, but he knew he couldn't: he could hardly walk anymore. Maybe if he ignored the call, the caller would be distracted.

'Hey! You with the sacks. Stop there! Stop!'

Jimmy stopped. When he stopped walking, he almost fell over. The weight of the sacks seemed to double when he stood still. The call had come from behind him, but he didn't turn around. He hadn't the strength.

Marching feet approached Jimmy from behind, the

sound of a squad of soldiers in army boots. Tears blurred Jimmy's vision still more. A heavy hand fell on his shoulder.

'Well,' said a Northern Irish accent. 'What have we here? I do believe it's our heroic wee Dubliner.'

It was the accent as much as the voice that Jimmy recognised. He turned in disbelief. He looked up into the big, scarred, friendly face of the sergeant who'd ordered him off Butt Bridge on Wednesday. Behind the sergeant a party of soldiers had come to a halt. Among them, grinning at him, Jimmy saw the faces of Jimmy Martin and the silver-haired corporal who'd collected the five shillings for him.

23

ACROSS THE LIFFEY

THE SERGEANT LOOKED DOWN at the pale boy in front of him. 'Still around, eh?' he asked.

Jimmy wondered at the change in the sergeant. In spite of his smile, he seemed subdued. Jimmy was so surprised even to see him that he forgot to answer his question. The sergeant gave a little laugh.

'Hard to get a word out of the wain,' he said to his men. 'I had the same trouble with him the first time I met him.'

'Please, sergeant,' Jimmy said. 'I'm sorry.'

'Did you see your relative, little man?' asked the silver-haired corporal.

Jimmy nodded, thinking quickly. Over the past few days he'd told so many versions of the truth that he wasn't sure any more which one he'd told the soldiers.

'Yes sir,' he said. 'I did.' He indicated the bulging sacks that weighed him down. 'I got all the food we need,' he said. 'But now I can't get it home.'

The soldiers smiled at him. They seemed able to ignore the storm of gunfire that was going on around them. But then, he supposed, soldiers must get used to gunfire. It was just part of their job. Da must be used to it now.

'You're still a game wee fellow anyhow,' said the corporal. 'You were heading back through the field of fire without a thought for your own skin.'

'Didn't I tell you he was a brave lad?' Martin asked proudly, as though any credit for such bravery was partly his. But Martin's voice sounded subdued too, and Jimmy noticed now that, under their smiles, all of these men looked very grim. 'Was it bad here?' he asked.

The big sergeant spat on the roadway. 'Not for us,' he said. 'But it was bad, aye. Bad for them poor swine in the Post Office. There were a lot of people shot, too, that had no part in this.'

Like all of them, he had to raise his voice to be heard above the shooting. He sounded almost angry. The other men looked uncomfortable.

'You can have some of this food, if you like,' Jimmy said. 'I'll have plenty for my family now.'

It was true enough. He could be generous now. He had a feeling this meeting was lucky for him. Besides, he felt he owed these men something. They'd been kind to him.

The sergeant looked silently at him for a while. Then he spat on the road again, as if trying to get a bad taste out of his mouth. He shook his head.

'No, son,' he said. 'We've been well fed. It's the people in your part of town who must be starving. If there's food left over, you give it to them.'

Again he looked at Jimmy, an odd, intense look. It was as though he were weighing the boy up in his own mind. Then he turned to his men.

'You, Martin,' he said. 'Take this boy across that river.'

It was what Jimmy had been hoping for, but the suddenness of it took his breath away. He'd been trying to think how he might persuade the soldiers to do this very thing. Now it was just happening.

Some part of Jimmy's mind resented the sudden stab of happiness that he felt. It resented his being so grateful to the enemy. But it wasn't these men, he thought, who were the enemy. They were just soldiers, like his Da. Maybe these Northerners didn't feel comfortable with what they were doing either.

Private Martin saluted the sergeant. The other soldiers

all wished Jimmy goodbye and good luck. He wished the same to them, really meaning it. Then Private Martin set off towards Tara Street, and Jimmy followed him without looking back.

'Well,' Martin said. 'Here we are again.'

'Yes,' said Jimmy. 'Going the other way.' It seemed strange that he should be returning as he'd come, with Private Martin leading him.

Tara Street was quiet. There were only a few soldiers there, and the guns in the tower of the fire station were silent. The area across the river was now in British hands.

From here Jimmy could see the smoking, gutted buildings at the Sackville Street end of Eden Quay. Some of them were still burning and black smoke and flames rose in the sky above Sackville Street.

'The whole street must be burning!' he said, awestruck. It was one thing to hear about it, another to see the flames with your own eyes. He'd been walking there only a few days ago.

'The south end of it anyway,' Martin said. He didn't sound pleased by the fact.

'What's wrong with the sergeant?' Jimmy asked him.

'The sergeant?' Martin frowned. 'Oh, I think some of us are wondering what we're doing here shooting at Irishmen and burning down Dublin.' He seemed to deliberately shrug off his unease. He looked at Jimmy and grinned. 'Well,' he said. 'You got your food, anyway. Your people should be all right now.'

Private Martin offered to carry the sacks for a while. Jimmy didn't want to part with them even for a second, but he told himself not to be an idiot. He eased the belt from around his neck and put the sacks on the ground. Private Martin picked them up and swung them across his shoulder.

'Good Lord!' he said, feeling the weight. 'How far have you carried these?'

'From Northumberland Road.'

The soldier grinned again. 'You know,' he said, 'you should join the army when you grow up. Carrying a full pack would be no bother to you.'

'No!' said Jimmy. 'I'll join no army!'

He regretted the words instantly. Private Martin might feel insulted. But to Jimmy's surprise the soldier nodded thoughtfully. 'Aye, lad,' he said. 'Maybe you're right.'

They crossed the river at Butt Bridge.

'I think I'll be all right from here,' Jimmy said.

Martin looked at him doubtfully, but nodded. 'Okay, old son,' he said. 'But go carefully.' He looked seriously at Jimmy for another long moment, then he smiled and winked.

'Up the rebels, eh Jimmy?' he whispered.

Jimmy summoned up strength to return the smile. 'Up the rebels, Jimmy,' he whispered back.

Martin put the sacks back on Jimmy's shoulders. They

seemed lighter now that he was close to home. Small and shabby though it might be, home called to him now in a voice that spoke of safety and peace – and a place to sleep for a very long time.

It was almost too easy now. Jimmy reached his own house without seeing a soul. The people of the slums, after five days of war, were cowering in their houses, hoping that the fighting would stop soon.

Jimmy struggled up the steps but had to rest again in the dark hallway before starting up the stairs. He'd run all the way from Marlborough Street, tired and laden though he was. He didn't know where he found the strength, but it was the last that he had.

He climbed the stairs very slowly, staggering with each step like a drunken man; but he didn't care. He only hoped he didn't pass out before reaching his own door.

When he finally reached his door he stood for a moment just looking at it, breathing heavily and swaying. He was listening. He heard no sound at all from the room beyond, not even a sigh.

The step forward that he took was less a step than a lurch. His hand, reaching for the doorhandle, didn't feel as if it belonged to him at all. It was numb. He had to struggle with the handle, and in the end he needed both hands to turn it. Then he staggered forward, pushing the door open as he fell into the room.

24

A VICTORY

JIMMY DROPPED TO THE FLOOR and lay there, looking up. Yes, there was the sagging bed, there was the big mattress. By the fireplace was his Ma's rocking chair. On the mantelpiece the old clock, the gateway to his daydreams, stood silent. Under its glass cover the hands on its face stood poised at five minutes to twelve, XI to XII. He was home.

Four people sat at the table and stared at him with wide eyes. For a long time neither he nor they moved nor spoke: they just looked at each other in shock.

Sarah and Josie stared open-mouthed at their brother, as though the sight of him frightened them. Beside them, Ma too looked fearful. Maybe they thought he was a ghost.

Ma looked very frail, her face lined with grief and worry, her skin pale. Her eyes were red from crying, the whiteness of her skin exaggerating the colour.

Ella, small and dark, sat beside her sister. She too had been crying. Marks of a beating stood out on her pale face.

'I'm back,' Jimmy said finally. 'I got food. I had fever but

I'm better. I couldn't get across the river before. I got the food from Ella's. Mrs Breen gave me cake ...'

The spell broke. Ma screamed, frightening Jimmy into silence. But it was a scream of joy, a scream in which he heard his own name. Ma jumped to her feet. Her chair fell, ignored, to the floor. She ran to her son and hugged him fiercely to her. She knelt down and put her head on his shoulder, sobbing with relief and happiness.

Over Ma's shoulder Jimmy saw the other three still staring. It was as though they knew that for now they had no part in this scene. This was between Jimmy and his Ma.

After a long time Ma stopped crying. She stood up and wiped her eyes with her apron, keeping one hand still on Jimmy's shoulder. It was as if she could only believe he was really there as long as she touched him. She looked closely at his face and saw the exhaustion there. She became suddenly cool and businesslike then, and when Jimmy tried to begin a faltering account of his adventures she hushed him instantly.

'Later,' she said. 'Tell me later. Rest now. You're worn out. Lie down,' she ordered, her 'policeman's voice' returning to her suddenly.

He didn't lie down so much as fall on to the mattress. He was still wearing all of his clothes, even his boots. For a moment he listened to the hum of voices as his aunt and sisters finally began to speak. They all started at once, chattering excitedly. Then Jimmy heard nothing, and saw nothing, but slept more deeply and more peacefully than he had ever done in the whole twelve years of his life.

Later, when Lily Conway came to look at him, she found that he was smiling in his sleep. She sat by his bed for a long time watching him, ignoring the excited whispers of the others as they examined the treasures he'd brought. The smile never left Jimmy's face.

Outside, the guns screamed their deadly messages into the falling dark. Buildings burned and crumbled into rubble, and men hunted each other in a deadly game whose outcome meant very little to her. Whoever might win, she would still live in a single tenement room and fend as best she could for her son and daughters. She had no choice but to wait, hoping for her husband's safe return from the bigger war, suspecting that if he did get back he would probably involve himself in this fresh fight.

Let men fight each other if they must: they always had, and Lily supposed they always would. She could see no sense in it herself. She too had a war to fight, but it was a war that made sense: the fight to feed her children and keep her family whole and safe. It was a secret war without any glory attached, a war just as old and just as dangerous as any fought by men, and the results of losing in that war were just as terrible.

The smiling boy sleeping now beside her had spent this week fighting in her war. Later, maybe, he'd join in the wars of men, though she hoped he would have more sense. But this time at least he'd enlisted in her army. She didn't need to know all the details of his adventures, though she was certain that she'd hear them all in time. She didn't even need to know what things he'd succeeded in bringing back. He'd gone out and done what he could, sickening her with worry; he'd come back bearing gifts, returning her to life. The most important thing was that he'd come back.

Ignoring the sounds of her sister and daughters, and the growling of the men's war that leaked in through the cracked window of the tenement room, Lily Conway smiled a smile that echoed her sleeping son's. Her son had been gone, and now he was returned to her. Tomorrow, things might be different; tomorrow, things might be better – or worse. That was the way of the world. But for this day at least, in the war that for her was the only real one, she had won.

Afterword

THE GENERAL POST OFFICE began to burn on that Friday, and was abandoned by the rebels on Friday evening. Trapped, they surrendered on Saturday. Pearse and Connolly signed an unconditional surrender order which was brought to all the remaining garrisons over the weekend. Jacob's biscuit factory, the last rebel stronghold to surrender, did so on Sunday, 30 April.

Over the next twelve days fourteen of the rebel leaders were tried by military courts and shot. Hundreds who'd taken part in the rebellion, and many who hadn't, were jailed or interned in Britain.

At first public opinion in Ireland was hostile to the rebels, but it was changed by the executions and reprisals. The internees, due mainly to international pressure, were released in 1917. Among the men released were Jimmy's uncle Mick and Paddy Doyle. They came back to find an Ireland where opinion had turned in their favour. To most people they were now heroes.

Jimmy's Da, James Conway, got out of the British army early in 1919. He'd been wounded twice in the war, but he recovered fully. On his return he found an Ireland that was quickly sliding into a war of its own, a war fought for independence. But that's another story.

Other books from
THE O'BRIEN PRESS

Also from Gerard Whelan

A WINTER OF SPIES

Eleven-year-old Sarah wants to be part
of the rebellion in Dublin in 1920. She
doesn't realise that her family already
plays an important role in Michael
Collins's spy ring, and that her actions
endanger them all. Sequel to the
award-winning *The Guns of Easter*.

WAR CHILDREN

A compelling and powerful collection
of stories set in the time of the War of
Independence. Six different children
try to come to terms with life during
wartime, a time when neither
ignorance nor innocence offer any
protection.

OUT OF NOWHERE

A young boy wakes up in a strange location. All he can remember is his own name, and all evidence of the outside world has seemingly been erased. What has happened? A thrilling and unpredictable adventure ...

DREAM INVADER

Saskia's uncle and aunt are worried about her little cousin, Simon, who is having terrible dreams. Something strange is definitely going on. Then an old woman enters the scene. The forces of good and evil fight for control over the child while Saskia watches the horrible events unfold ...

HISTORICAL NOVELS

KATIE'S WAR
Aubrey Flegg

Katie's father returns shellshocked from the Great War. Four years later another war is breaking out, this time the Civil War in Ireland. Katie's family is split by divided loyalties, and she feels there is no way she can help. Then she and the Welsh boy, Dafydd, find a hidden arms cache. Can they make a difference after all?

FARAWAY HOME
Marilyn Taylor

Two Jewish children, Karl and Rosa, escape from Nazi-occupied Austria on board a *Kindertransport*. Their new home is a refugee farm in Northern Ireland. Here, they must learn to cope with the absence of their loved ones. Will they ever see their family again?

Based on the true story of Millisle refugee farm in Ards, County Down.

HISTORICAL BIOGRAPHY

STRONGBOW
The Story of Richard and Aoife
Morgan Llywelyn

An action-packed tale of the famous Norman knight who captured Dublin and married an Irish princess, Aoife, the King of Leinster's daughter.

RED HUGH
The Kidnap of Hugh O'Donnell
Deborah Lisson

Red Hugh O'Donnell, son of the leader of the powerful O'Donnell clan, is captured by the English authorities and detained in Dublin Castle. His bid to survive records an unforgettable episode in Irish, and English, history.

PIRATE QUEEN
Morgan Llywelyn

Grace O'Malley, pirate and trader, is one of Ireland's most infamous figures. A thorn in the side of the English administration, she lived an extraordinary, adventure-filled life. This is the story of a remarkable woman who broke the mould.

From Eoin Colfer

BENNY AND OMAR

A hilarious book in which young sporting fanatic Benny is forced to leave his beloved Wexford, home of all his hurling heroes, and move with his family to Tunisia! How will he survive in a place like this? Then he teams up with Omar, and a madcap friendship between the two boys leads to trouble, crazy escapades, a unique way of communicating and much more.

BENNY AND BABE

Benny is visiting his grandfather in the country for the summer holidays and finds his position as a 'townie' makes him the object of much teasing by the natives. He's able to give as good as he gets – until he meets Babe, the village tomboy, and in this cool customer he meets his match. When the two get mixed up with Furty Howlin, things become very complicated – and dangerous.

From Siobhán Parkinson

SISTERS ... NO WAY!

Cindy, a with-it and cynical young teen, still traumatised by her mother's recent death, is appalled when her father falls in love with one of her teachers, a woman with two prissy teenage daughters. Surely he can't be serious? She is *never* going to call them sisters ... no way! As for the 'prissy' girls, they think Cindy is an absolute horror – spoiled, arrogant and rude. They can't imagine being landed with Cindy as a sister ... no way! An amusing and touching story about change and growing up.

FOUR KIDS, THREE CATS, TWO COWS, ONE WITCH (maybe)

Beverley, a bit of a snob, cooks up a plot to visit the island off the coast. She manages to convince the somewhat cautious Elizabeth and her cousin, Gerard, to go with her. Then there's a surprise companion – Kevin, the cool guy who works in the local shop. This motley crew must find ways to support each other, and put up with each other's shortcomings, when they are stranded on the island and encounter a strange inhabitant.

AMELIA

The year is 1914 and Amelia Pim will soon be thirteen. There are rumours of war and rebellion, and Dublin is holding its breath for a major upheaval. But all that matters to Amelia is what she will wear to her birthday party. Then disaster strikes the Pim family. Mama's political activities bring disgrace, and it is Amelia who must hold the family together. Only the friendship of the servant girl, Mary Ann, seems to promise any hope.

NO PEACE FOR AMELIA

It's 1916, but Amelia Pim's thoughts are on Frederick Goodbody and not on the war in Europe. Then Frederick enlists. The pacifist Quaker community is shocked, but Amelia is secretly proud of her hero and goes to the quayside to wave him farewell. For her friend, Mary Ann, there are problems too, with her brother's involvement in the Easter Rising. What will become of the two young men and what effect will it have on the lives of Amelia and Mary Ann